VAMPIRE HIGH
SOPHOMORE YEAR

VAMPIRE HIGH

SOPHOMORE YEAR

DOUGLAS REES

DELACORTE PRESS

All rights reserved. Published in the United States by Delacorte Press, an imprint of Random House Children's Books, a division of Random House, Inc., New York.

Delacorte Press is a registered trademark and the colophon is a trademark of Random House, Inc.

Visit us on the Web! www.randomhouse.com/kids

Educators and librarians, for a variety of teaching tools, visit us at www.randomhouse.com/teachers.

Library of Congress Cataloging-in-Publication Data
Rees, Douglas.
Vampire High : sophomore year / Douglas Rees. — 1st ed.
p. cm.
Summary: When Cody's Goth cousin Turk moves into his house, enrolls at Vlad Dracul, and decides to turn an abandoned nineteenth-century mill into an art center, the vampire (jenti) students are not pleased, and Cody's hopes for a great sophomore year are blighted.
ISBN 978-0-385-73725-8 (hc: alk. paper)—ISBN 978-0-385-90657-9 (glb: alk. paper)—ISBN 978-0-375-89665-1 (e-book) [1. Vampires—Fiction. 2. High schools—Fiction. 3. Schools—Fiction. 4. Artists—Fiction. 5. Goth culture (Subculture)—Fiction. 6. Massachusetts—Fiction.] I. Title.
PZ7.R25475Vd 2010
[Fic]—dc22
2009027168

The text of this book is set in 12.5-point Apollo MT.

Book design by Angela Carlino

Printed in the United States of America

10 9 8 7 6 5 4 3 2 1

First Edition

For Laurie McLean,

who makes things happen

I

It was one of those hot, sticky Massachusetts August nights when it doesn't cool off. The sky was full of thunderheads, and the hills around New Sodom echoed the roaring, grumbling air. It was the kind of night when witches might be out, casting their shadows in the glare of lightning bolts.

Which made it a perfect time for my cousin to show up.

My mom and dad were asleep upstairs. I was sitting up watching an old horror movie called *The Bride of Frankenstein*. Maybe you've seen it. The monster's back, and he wants good old Dr. Frankenstein to make him a girlfriend so he won't be so lonely. So Doc F. gets back into his mysterious lab and splices together a lady monster out of whatever parts he's got lying around. The movie had reached the scene where the new monster-lady has just opened her eyes and started to walk around. She's staring, moving slowly, not certain of anything. Then she sees her fiancé and hisses. She raises a hand that you know has to have claws instead of nails, and you know the big guy's plans for happiness in a little rose-covered dungeon somewhere are not going to happen.

It's a really tense scene, and when a crack of thunder went off in what sounded like our attic, I jumped a foot, even though I'd seen the movie before.

Then, as the thunder died away, I heard the rain start to come down, hard.

And then came the knock on the door.

When you hear a knock on the door at one in the morning, you know it's not good news, whatever it is. So I waited until it came a second time, figuring maybe it would go away. I mean, I didn't really think there was a monster out there. I was almost sixteen. I knew there was no such thing. Vampires, sure. New Sodom is full of them. Like they say, some of my best friends are vampires. But even so, why would one of them be banging on our door in the middle of the night?

The knock came again, hard and heavy, and I knew I'd have to answer it. I knew because my father called down, "For God's sake, Cody, see who it is."

I paused the movie and went to the door.

The thunder rolled again, farther away now. The storm was moving fast.

"Who is it?" I asked.

No answer.

"Justin?" I whispered. "Ileana?" I figured it might be my

best friend or my girl, though it wasn't like them to come calling past midnight. Still, they were vampires—jenti, I mean. And while jenti don't really burn up when the sun hits them, they do like nighttime.

I heard the sound of something scratching on the door. Scratching slowly, as if whatever was doing it took pleasure in the sound. Scratching as if there might be some invisible crevice wide enough to force a set of claws through. And there was only one person I knew who would ever do that.

"Raquel?" I said, and opened the door.

She stood there in the harsh glow of the porch light, tall, thin, pale, dressed in black leather. Her dark hair was cropped short, the nails she'd scratched the door with were pointed and black, and she had a gold stud shaped like a skull in her left nostril.

"Hi, Cuz," she said. "Ya gonna let me in?"

"What are you doing here?" I squeaked. "You're not supposed to be here for another week."

"Okay. I'll just camp out here until you're ready for me," she said. "You gonna let me use the bathroom, or would you rather I pee in the bushes? Either way's good."

"Get in here," I said.

"Before the vampires get me?" she said. "Where are they, anyway?"

"Just get in here," I said between clenched teeth.

She shouldered past me into the foyer and said, "Thanks. By the way, don't call me Raquel again. I'm Turquoise now."

"Turquoise," I said. "Turquoise Stone. I'll be sure to remember."

"Turk for short."

"Whatever."

My mom and dad were coming down the stairs.

"Rachel, darling," Mom said, and practically flew across the room to hug and kiss my cousin. "How did you get here so soon?" she asked. "Is everything all right at home?"

"No," Turk said. "It never is."

"Hello, Rachel," Dad said, standing on the stairs. "Or is it still Raquel?"

"I haven't been either one for a while," Turk said.

"It's Turquoise," I said. "Turk for short."

"Right," Dad said.

"I'm being forced to stay with you anyway," Turk said. "So I thought, 'Why let Mom stuff me in a plane at her convenience?' And I drove."

"You have a car?" I said.

"That's what people usually drive," Turk said.

This interested me. I would be driving soon myself. I had been thinking a lot about cars.

"What have you got?" I asked.

"It's at the curb," Turk said. "The black thing."

Under the streetlight, I saw a shiny black Volkswagen Bug, the old kind.

"You drove all the way from Seattle?" Mom said. "You must have seen some interesting sights."

"I drive at night," Turk said. "I hate scenery. It's distracting."

She unslung her coat. Her arms were bare under it, and I could see the reason that dear, sweet Turk had come to live with our happy family. Her tattoo. Turk had a pale blue two-headed snake that began at her wrists, wrapped around her arms, and (according to Mom's sister, Aunt Imelda) ran across her back.

"Spiffy," Dad said. "Best illegal tattoo I've ever seen."

"It wasn't illegal in Mexico." Turk shrugged. "And it's my body."

I had to admit, I was impressed. Even if it was the thing that had made Aunt Imelda decide that she couldn't even pretend to control Rachel/Raquel/Turquoise/Turk anymore, and send her to us. A couple of weeks before, when she and Turk had been on vacation in Acapulco, my cousin had gotten off her leash and headed straight for a tattoo parlor. When Aunt Imelda finally caught up with her, she was just getting the last snake head done, while a bunch of guys from the Mexican Navy stood around admiring her courage.

She had been missing for a week. Tattoos like that take a lot of time.

So now here she was, ready to envelop us all in her own special aura.

"Did it hurt much?" Mom asked.

"Sure," Turk said. "That was the point."

There wasn't much to say to that, so Mom changed the subject.

"Jack, Cody. Bring in Rach—Turk's things."

"I've got 'em," Turk said. She picked up an old army duffel bag and a sleeping bag. That was about half of what she'd brought. The rest was some boxes of art supplies, some canvases, an easel, and an inflated doll. The doll's mouth was open and its hands were raised to its face. I recognized it from a famous painting called *The Scream*.

"You don't have to help me," Turk said. "Just show me where I sleep. I'll come back for the other stuff."

"Come upstairs, dear. I'll show you your room," Mom said, and gestured for us to pick up the things on the porch.

Mom and Turk went up the stairs.

"What is that object?" Dad said, looking at the doll.

"It's called *The Scream,*" I said.

"I know that, but what *is* it?" Dad said.

"Maybe she sleeps with it," I said to Dad as he tucked it under his arm.

"Then no wonder it's screaming," he said.

We went upstairs with our arms full of stuff.

"I'm afraid it's not really ready," Mom was saying about the room. "I was planning to start work on it tomorrow."

It looked ready to me. There were white curtains and a double bed with a white bedspread, and an antique chest of drawers, a desk, and a chair. For a girl, it seemed great.

"Don't bother," Turk said. "I can design my own space. You have an attic, right?"

"Yes," Mom said.

"It's huge," I said.

"How do I get up there?" Turk asked.

"There's a trapdoor with a ladder in the hall," Dad said.

"Cool," Turk said.

So we followed her into the hall.

"There's nothing up there, you know," Mom told her. "Just some old boxes."

Turk jumped up and grabbed the cord that pulled down the ladder. The ladder swung down with a screech. Then she slithered up the steps.

"Perfect," she announced. "I'll sleep here."

"But it's awful up there," Mom said.

"I'm into that," Turk said. "Just hand me up my stuff."

"It's dusty. There are only two small windows. I don't think it's healthy," Dad said. "I'm going to have to put my foot down, Turk."

"Put it anywhere you want, Uncle Jack," Turk said. "But the CO_2 level in the atmosphere is already higher than it's been in a hundred thousand years. Every breath we take is choking us. So what's a little dust?"

"Is she staying with us forever?" Dad whispered to Mom.

"It's gonna seem like it," I said.

"Turk, sleep down here tonight, and I'll help you sweep it out tomorrow," Mom called up.

"Give me a broom and I'll sweep it out now," Turk said. "It won't take more than half an hour."

"It's after one in the morning," Dad said.

"Go back to bed. I don't need any help," Turk said.

"Why don't we let her do it?" Mom said to Dad. "There's no point in getting into a screaming fight right now."

I put down Turk's stuff and went and got a broom and dustpan.

"Thanks," she said when I handed them up. "You can just drop my stuff. I'll get it when I'm done. Good night, guys. Thanks for having me."

Dad dropped the duffel bag and the inflated doll. *The Scream* bounced across the floor and ended up in the corner, tilted back and looking up at the top of the steps, where Turk had started to sweep.

"I know how you feel," I said to the doll.

We all went into the kitchen. Mom put on the teakettle.

"St.-John's-wort tea," she said. "It'll help us get back to sleep."

"Give me plenty," Dad said. "I don't want to wake up for the next few years."

"It's a good thing we're doing," Mom said. "It's a necessary thing. It's an obligation. We're family. She and Imelda are at daggers drawn, and they need a break from each other.

And Rachel—Turk—needs a new start. Moving in with us is the best chance she has."

Dad looked up at the ceiling. Then he looked at me.

"All very true, and I will do my best to be a good uncle," Dad said. "But Cody, my son, when the time comes for you to marry, promise you'll give serious consideration to the advantages of birth control."

2

I finished my movie and went to bed.

Lying there, I could hear Turk over my head, sweeping and moving things around. Since I couldn't sleep, I remembered things about my cousin.

When I was seven and she was eight, she turned an old water heater into a spaceship. She painted it silver and cut out cardboard fins and stuck them on with duct tape. I mean, it was amazing work for an eight-year-old. Anyway, it amazed me.

And when she told me I could be an astronaut and go with her to the moon, I was ready. She even gave me her special Space Ranger Galaxy III helmet to wear.

"I've already been a couple of times," she said. "It's really easy if you know what you're doing."

So I climbed into the spaceship and lay there up by the nose, which was a cone of really heavy poster board, also painted silver.

Nothing happened. I just lay there, feeling more and more cramped and sweaty, watching my Galaxy III helmet's faceplate start steaming up, feeling the oxygen going bye-bye.

I started to wonder: Had I already started? Was I in outer space? Why wasn't there a window in this thing?

Then the spaceship was rocked by a cosmic bang. Then a horrible smell filled the helmet. I was crashing, I was burning, I was going to die.

I started to thrash around, rocking the ship, which just scared me more. And without thinking about it, just trying to get away from that horrible smell, I pushed myself forward and burst through the paper nose cone. When I got out, I took off running. I ran across the backyard, around the house, and up to the corner before I realized I was safe, and back on planet Earth.

I took off the good old Galaxy III. I breathed in the best air I'd ever breathed. I turned my face to the sun, and without thinking about it, I said, "Hi!"

Then I heard the sound of angry voices coming from Turk's backyard. I walked back to find out what was going on.

I still remember Dad saying, "Where is Cody? What have you done with my son?"

It's kind of a warm memory, actually. But not as warm as the memory of Number 3, Aunt Imelda's husband of the year, turning Turk over his knee and paddling her.

He stopped when I came closer and said, "Let me, Uncle Jeff, let me!"

Then for two minutes it was all about Cody. Was I all right? What had happened? What had we been playing?

"I went to outer space," I said. "But I didn't like it."

The spaceship looked like it had had a rough trip. The nose cone was ripped, of course. And the back end was blackened and smoking. A long electric cord ran from the house to a battery charger, the kind they have in repair garages, which Number 3 owned a couple of. The battery charger was hooked up to a battery surrounded by six other batteries, and those batteries were connected to each other by a few twists of copper wire. The spaceship's engine, of course.

What had happened was that Turk had tried to charge the batteries all at once, off the one charger. The one in the center had heated up enough to blow the caps off the cells. That was the sound I had heard, echoing in the spaceship. The bad smell had been the cloud of sulfuric acid that rolled out of the battery once the caps had blown.

"How high did I get?" I wanted to know.

Turk explained everything. Of course she hadn't tried out her spaceship herself. How could she start the engine if she was inside? Why hadn't she told me I was the test pilot? Because if she had, maybe I wouldn't have done what she wanted. It all made perfect sense.

We went home, and we didn't get together with them again until Aunt Imelda was on husband Number 4.

By that time, I was ten and Turk was eleven. This time, it was she and Aunt Imelda and Number 4 who came to visit us. I figured I was safe enough on my own turf. I mean, she couldn't bring her latest spaceship, or whatever she was working on, with her. So I was kind of looking forward to the visit, the way kids do. You figure, you've got a cousin coming, someone new to play with. Right?

Right. But the only game she wanted to play was Kidnapper, where she tied me up and left me in my own tree house for about twelve hours, until Dad climbed up and got me down. Why hadn't I at least called for help? I had. But no one had heard me. Probably because of the gag in my mouth.

"Sorry, Cody," she said the next morning. "I didn't mean to leave you out there. I just sort of forgot."

Then, when she had turned thirteen and Aunt Imelda had moved to Seattle and was revving up husband Number 6, we heard that Turk had become an artist. She sketched. She painted. She hammered together weird things out of hunks of wood. She wore a black T-shirt that said DESPAIR IS GOOD FOR YOU, and it was the only shirt she would wear. Aunt Imelda had to get her a dozen or she wouldn't change.

Last year, when I'd been getting started here at Vlad Dracul Magnet School, she'd entered an art contest. Her art was a black urinal turned upside down. The title was *Homage to Marcel Duchamp.*

Aunt Imelda sent us a copy of the program. Under "*Homage to Marcel Duchamp,* Raquel Stone, Age 16" was the explanation of why this was Art.

"As Duchamp exhibited a urinal to express his rage and despair at the slaughter of World War I, and the inadequacy of language to describe it, this work expresses rage and despair at Duchamp's inability to express his rage and despair adequately."

First prize. Five thousand dollars.

"You could redo a whole bathroom for that," Dad said when he read it. "With plenty left over for toilet paper."

Instead, Turk bought her car, and we heard it got to be pretty well known around Seattle. Partly this was because it was always shiny black no matter what the weather was like. Partly this was because she drove it on her learner's permit and the cops kept stopping her.

Meanwhile, she won another prize. This one for a piece called *Daddy Six*. It was photographs of all the guys Aunt Imelda had married, wrapped up in a net of rusty barbed wire.

Along with the prize, she got a free trip to a girls' school in Arizona for troubled teens, which was Number 6's idea. She was there about three weeks. Then the school sent her back with a note asking Aunt Imelda to please try somewhere else. Turk had organized the girls into a union and led them out on strike.

Now here she was in strange old New Sodom, where maybe half the population was vampires—I mean, jenti—and until a couple of months ago, nobody had ever talked about it. Not the jenti, not the gadje—which was what the jenti called us. They had lived side by side all their lives and never spoken of what everyone knew. That vampires were real. That they clustered in New Sodom. That they had been here from the beginning.

Things were more out in the open now. Things that nobody had admitted for three hundred years. But a lot of people thought things had been better the old way. And some of them probably blamed me for what I had done to change things.

So I could hardly wait to see what my cousin was going to do to me now that we were living together in the weirdest little city in America.

3

The next morning, late, I got up to a wet, cloudy day. The air was full of a sense that some nameless awfulness was going to happen. I wondered if my cousin brought her own weather with her.

Mom made me breakfast, which was nice of her. Then she said, "I was hoping you could introduce Turk to some of your friends today," which was not so nice. But it had to happen sooner or later. Justin and Ileana and all the other jenti who'd become my friends were over quite a bit. Eventually, they were going to notice that our house was being haunted.

I figured I'd start with Ileana, because she was my girl-friend. And because she was a jenti princess. Which meant she knew how to be polite to anybody.

When I called Ileana, she said she'd be happy to come over. And she'd bring Justin. Which was maybe for the best. Maybe meeting Turk with Ileana here would kind of lessen the shock for him.

"Whatever," Turk said when I told her. "Are they some of your vampire friends?"

"None of my friends are vampires," I told her. "They're jenti. *Vampire* is kind of an insult."

"Whatever," Turk said.

"No, really, Turk. If you're going to live in New Sodom, you have to know what it's like here," I said. "There are the jenti and the gadje. That's everybody who's not jenti. And the V-word is not used unless you want to get someone mad."

"I don't care whether I get anybody mad or not," Turk said.

"Well, I do," I said.

"I know you're some kind of big hero to them," Turk said. "Congratulations. But you'll have to forgive me if I don't join in the worship."

"Who told you I'm a hero?" I asked.

"My mom. She heard it from your mom. Isn't it true?"

"Here's what's true," I said. "I started at Vlad last winter after I basically got thrown out of Cotton Mather High across town. That was the gadje school. Dad put me into Vlad because it had such a great academic reputation, and it was supposed to be tough.

"Well, I thought they wouldn't take me because of my lousy record at Cotton Mather. But they only asked one question: Was I willing to play water polo? I said sure, figuring I'd try out for the team and get rejected. I'd still be at Vlad, Dad would be off my back, it would all be cool.

"Only it turned out that the water polo team was kind of a scam. They only had one because the state required it for accreditation. Since jenti can't swim, they recruited a few gadje and let them fool around in the water. They lost every game, and nobody cared."

"And you were the big jock hero who said, 'Come on, boys, let's win one for the Flipper'?" Turk said.

"No," I said. "When I found out what was going on—pretend to play water polo for a few years and get As without working and get accepted to some college where the jenti run things—I thought I was in heaven for about a day. Then I thought about how much contempt they must have for us to treat us like that, and I got mad. So I started trying to do the work. The teachers, and the principal, Horvath, didn't like that. They wanted their gadje lazy and stupid. But I made a couple of friends who helped me. Justin Warrener and Ileana Antonescu. Justin explained all kinds of stuff about how things work in the jenti world, and in New Sodom. Ileana—"

I took a breath.

"She marked me. She did it to save me from getting beaten up by some guys who were going to throw Justin in a creek. As a marked gadje, I was her private blood supply, and none of them could touch me."

"And she did this because . . . ," Turk said.

"I tried to stop the guys who were going to dunk Justin. Water can do very bad things to jenti. Only there were four of them and one of me. Plus, they were jenti. Stronger than we are." I twitched, still remembering how they'd bounced me around like a soccer ball until Ileana showed up.

"Sweet," Turk said.

"And Justin explained what was going on. I didn't know that I was in a high school full of jenti. I didn't know real jenti existed. Anyway, we got to be friends. And they both helped me with my work until I got good enough to make Cs. Without them, I'd never have survived last semester," I said.

"I'm still waiting to hear the part where you're a hero," Turk said.

"It's not that big a deal," I said. "Well, it was to them. But all I did was give Justin a blood transfusion. Ileana was having her fifteenth birthday party, which is a major event to the jenti, and I was at the party feeling really out of it without him. I was probably the first gadje ever to get invited to something like that, and a lot of the jenti didn't want me there. So I called to find out when he was coming. Justin couldn't be there because, well, because he needed more blood than the average jenti and they were out at his house. The Warreners don't have a lot of money. So I asked Ileana for permission to go over and give him a drink. Well, this turned out to be a huge thing to the jenti. It's like, they have all this folklore about the kind gadje who just gives blood without asking for anything in return, and by the time Justin and I got to the party, everyone knew what I'd done."

"So where does the water polo come in?"

"That was Justin more than me," I said. "In fact, it was all Justin, really. He was hanging out at the pool with me, just the two of us, and all of a sudden he jumped into the water. Well, I almost freaked. I mean, here's my best friend, and he's just dived into something that can kill him. Only he doesn't die. He changes. Into something like a seal. They call it a selkie. Turns out that little jenti like him, the ones with the brown hair and blue eyes, can't fly or turn into wolves, but they can survive in water. No, not survive. They love it. So we just recruited a new water polo team from the selkie jenti and the state had to let us stay open."

"Why did the state want to close you down?" Turk asked.

"We hadn't met our minimum number of games for the year when Justin beat up the old team," I said. "And some of them quit."

"Justin. The little guy. All by himself. Beat up the team," Turk said.

"I said he was little, I didn't say he was weak," I said. "There's no such thing as a weak jenti."

"But why did he do it?"

"They were beating me up," I said.

Turk pretended to brush away a tear. "I'm all choked up," she said.

"Do you want to hear this stuff or not?" I said.

"Oh, yes, please," Turk said. "Only get to the good part."

"There isn't much more," I said. "We trained the selkie team in secret, then we all showed up for the last game, and we got into the water. By the end of the game, the gym was full. Everyone in the school was watching. Even Dracula. Of course, I didn't know it was Dracula then. Nobody but Horvath did. We thought he was just this big wolf the school kept around as a mascot."

For the first time, Turk looked impressed.

"You know Dracula?"

"I just met him once for a minute," I said. "Of course, he showed me around the school the first day. But that was when I thought he was just a wolf."

"When do I meet him?" Turk asked.

"I don't know," I said. "He decided to stop being a wolf at the end of the year and took off for Europe. He'll probably be back, though. Ileana is one of his descendants, and she's important to him."

Turk closed her eyes.

"Oh, Cody," she said. "So noble. So brave."

"I had a busy semester," I agreed. And I resisted adding, "And I was looking forward to the next one. Until you showed up."

4

Mom turned dinner into a big deal. Ileana and Justin were invited. Which gave her the rest of the day to cook, which she loved to do, and gave me the rest of the day to worry.

As for Turk, once she had swilled a few cups of coffee, she went back to her attic, pulled the steps up after her, and made more noise. It was hard to tell what she might be doing up there, but the sounds moved all over the second floor ceiling.

"You know, I really feel like a total New Englander now," Dad said as the gray light dimmed and dinnertime heaved into view. "We've got a two-hundred-year-old house in a nearly four-hundred-year-old town, a wood-burning stove in the kitchen, birch trees in the yard, and now—a crazy relative in the attic. Perhaps we ought to chain her up."

I shook my head. "Good luck trying," I said.

Exactly at six, a limousine purred up to the curb behind the little black Volkswagen, and Ileana and Justin got out.

Just seeing Ileana made me glow inside. We'd been together for four months now, and things kept on getting better and better between us. Sometimes, I could hardly believe that this beautiful little girl really liked me better than the jenti boys she could have had. She just came up to my shoulders—sometimes jenti are small—and she was perfect. Shining black hair, an ivory-pale face with glowing brown eyes, and lips like the bow on a present waiting to be unwrapped.

As for Justin and me—best friends. Enough said.

They came up the walk together, Ileana in a little black dress and Justin in a dark suit. I kind of wished they hadn't gone to so much trouble for Turk. But that's the jenti way. All out, whatever they're doing. There's no such thing as a casual jenti.

Ileana danced into the house, looking cool even on this muggy evening. She gave me a kiss on the cheek.

"Look at Justin," she said. "He has become a Mercian."

"A what?" I said.

I looked more closely at Justin's coat and saw he was wearing a two-headed silver eagle on it. There was a crown balancing on both the eagle's heads, and under its feet was the word MERCIA.

"Neat," I said. "What's a Mercian?"

"Just a kind of old jenti thing," Justin said quietly. "I was invited to join."

"He was invited to join because of you," Ileana said. "Because you and he saved the school."

Justin shrugged.

"So what do you do?" I asked.

"Oh, just talk about stuff here in town," he said.

"It is more than that," Ileana said. "Only certain families may belong. Even my father could not join, because he is not out of the Mercian line. And to be invited to join so young never happens."

"Well, congratulations," I said.

Sitting around with some old guys talking about New Sodom did not sound like much of an honor to me, even if it was secret and ancient and all that other jenti stuff, but if Justin was happy, I was happy.

Ileana handed me a small box wrapped in white paper and silver ribbon.

"For your cousin," she said. "Please give it to her tonight."

She flashed a smile that showed her cute little fangs.

"Oops," she said, and covered her mouth. "They are out, are they not? Excuse me. I must be a little excited."

"Don't be," I said. "My cousin—"

"Of course I am excited," Ileana said. "This is the first of your relatives I have ever met, apart from your parents."

Jenti are big on family. But then, when your reunions are attended by people who've been alive since the fifteenth century, relatives probably seem a lot more important.

"Thanks for having us over so soon," Justin said, and handed me a small package wrapped in brown paper and blue ribbon. "This is for your cousin, too."

"Why don't you give her these?" I asked.

"Because you are the connection between us," Ileana said. "If I give something directly to your relative on our first meeting, it is a great insult to you."

"Like cutting you out," Justin said.

Jenti manners are only slightly less complicated than their special language, which even most of them don't speak well anymore.

"Well, thanks," I said. "Let's go into the dining room."

Mom and Dad were already there. I noticed Dad had his wineglass in hand. Lucky Dad. All I had was the certainty that Turk was going to do something to show us how little we all meant to her.

Then Turk made her entrance.

She was barefoot, and wearing paint-smeared black jeans and one of her T-shirts. There was a lot of paint on her, too, most of it black. I wondered how much time she'd spent decorating herself.

"Oh. Hi," she said. "Sorry. Didn't know it was so late."

Like Mom hadn't told her twenty times to start getting ready.

Ileana and Justin both smiled. This time, without fangs.

"Welcome, kinswoman to Cody," Ileana said. Then she added something in jenti that means "Rest beneath the shadow of my wings," which is a huge compliment to a gadje, especially one you've just met.

"Hello," Justin said.

"So you guys are vampires, right?" Turk said.

Polite. I was going to be polite. I could always kill my cousin later.

"These are for you from Ileana and Justin," I said, handing Turk the boxes.

"What? Do I open them now?" Turk said.

"It might make it easier to say thank you if you knew what was in them," I said.

"Sure. Whatever," Turk said.

She opened the one from Ileana first.

Inside was a turquoise pendant set in silver and hanging from a chain.

It was fun to watch cousin Turk just then. She wanted to look so unimpressed. And she couldn't.

"It's Hopi," Turk said. "Classic Hopi."

"From Cochiti Pueblo," Ileana said.

Turk turned the jewel in her hands.

"Nobody's doing this kind of work anymore," she said.

"My grandfather brought it home from one of his trips," Ileana said. "His friend Kit Carson gave it to him. That is the story in the family."

Turk put the jewel back in the box. Carefully.

"Well. Thanks," she said.

Then she opened Justin's box.

Inside was a folded-up piece of paper.

"This is kind of a certificate," Turk read. "It's good for any two of my angelfish, any kind you might like. I can help you set them up. I have plenty of spare aquarium stuff, and can give you plenty of tubifex worms. They really go for tubifex worms as a supplement. Welcome to New Sodom, Justin Warrener."

Turk gave him a thin little smile.

"Thanks, man," she said. "But I kill fish. Goldfish see me coming and they turn belly-up. Neon tetras commit mass suicide. Guppies eat themselves. I don't want to ice a couple of your pets."

"Bet I could help you keep 'em alive," Justin said.

"Justin knows everthing about angelfish," I said. "He's got a room full of them. He sells them all over the country."

"If you like angelfish," Justin added.

"They don't fit with my lifestyle," Turk said. "Thanks anyway."

"Oh. Okay," Justin said.

I cringed inside.

Dad rolled his eyes.

"Let's have dinner," Mom said.

Mom had gotten out the best china. There was a French soup that would have been good enough for the dining room at Vlad, and quiche and salad. Dad had spent all day caramelizing his patented flan for dessert.

Ileana and I sat across from Turk and Justin, with Mom and Dad at the ends of the table. There were flowers and candles.

In the flickering light, I couldn't help noticing how much more my cousin looked like a typical jenti than Justin did. He was short and brown-haired like most of the old New England jenti. Dark and rangy Turk in her black-on-black-on-black ensemble could have slouched down the hall at Vlad Dracul without getting a second look, except for her paint and tattoo.

We got through the soup and salad all right. Mom and Dad and I talked with Justin and Ileana mostly. We tried to include Turk, but most of her answers were shrugs. That suited me. I hoped she wouldn't say more than three complete sentences, one of which would be "Good night." But it was not to be.

"So, you'll be going to school with us?" Justin said when we were starting on the flan.

"Yeah, I guess," Turk said. "If I like it. If not—" She shrugged.

"What will happen if you do not?" Ileana wanted to know.

"Drop out, grab my stuff, head for Europe," Turk said. "Or back to Mexico. Doesn't matter. I won't be staying long anyplace from now on. But, yeah. I'll go to school until then. The only reason I agreed to come here was to try out Vlad."

"We are so glad you did," Ileana said. "Cody has found it quite interesting."

"Interesting and hard," I said.

"Hard," Turk said. "Well, let's face it, Cuz. I'm the one with the brains in our little duo."

I could tell this was going to be a dinner party I'd remember for years to come.

"Cody's smart enough," Justin said, which may not have sounded like a ringing endorsement of my intelligence but meant a lot in Justin-speak.

"Perhaps you'd like to tell Justin and Ileana about your art," Mom said.

"No," Turk said. "There's no point in talking about it."

"I would be very interested to hear," Ileana said.

"Sure would," Justin agreed.

"It's personal," Turk said. "But I'll tell you what I would be interested in talking about. I'd be interested to hear about being a vampire."

"Hey," I said. "I told you about that word."

"That's what interests me," Turk said. "One of the things. If it's what you are, why not use it? It's just a word."

"Just a word," Justin said.

"As a lawyer, I know something about words," Dad said. "They're weapons."

I could feel the tension building in the room. Most of it was mine. But there was enough to go around.

"I will try to answer your question," Ileana said in her softest, most polite voice. "It is, as you say, only a word. But it is the word by which your people burned, and slew, and persecuted mine for thousands of years. Not without reason. We were blood-drinkers, and we still are. And in the days before it was possible to store blood against the times when we would need it, we would do anything we could in order to get it. We paid in gold for a little blood from a willing gadje. And if no willing gadje could be found, we took what we needed anyway. And around this terrible need you wove a black wreath of stories of our greed, our ruthlessness, our magical powers, and used it to strengthen your hatred. Still, we managed to live among you. We were human beings, after all. We hid ourselves in plain sight, made alliances with some of you when we could. But always the need, and the fear of the need, our fear of it and yours, was there. And this was almost yesterday. Less than two hundred years ago were we able to feed ourselves without violence for the first time. Things are better now. We are trying to change. But the word *vampire* makes us remember in our bones all the dark years when to be one of us was to be cursed. Perhaps that is why we do not think it is friendly to use it."

"Stake through the heart, you know?" Justin said. "There are places in this town where that happened."

His hand went to the silver eagle on his lapel.

"Fantastic," Turk said. And if I hadn't known better, I would have sworn she sounded excited. Maybe even happy. "Do you guys want to see my art?"

Justin, Ileana, and I all looked at each other. We couldn't say no now without being as rude as she'd been.

"Yes," Ileana said.

Turk stood up.

"Let's go up to my place," she said.

We all followed her up to the attic. What had been the attic. It was on the way to being something else now. A studio, a room, a private world, maybe. Anyway, you sure knew Turk was there.

The windows had been covered with newspapers. A painting was propped in each one. The boxes had been shifted around and turned into a kind of sofa and a couple of chairs. Turk's sleeping bag was unrolled on the sofa. In one corner, another box, turned on its side, held her clothes, neatly stacked up, with *The Scream* beside it. Her easel was in another corner. And running along the length of the ceiling was a long black tissue paper snake with two heads.

"I like it," Dad said, looking around. "Kind of light and airy. Feminine touch. Comfy."

"The Snake of Life," Ileana said, looking up at the paper snake. "The jenti tell stories about this creature."

"Yeah," Turk said. "But this is like the Aztec version. It turns up in their culture, too."

Ileana nodded.

"Beginning and end. Not to be defeated or destroyed," Ileana said. "That is what it means to us."

"Not to mention the extra fangs," Turk said.

"Is that tissue paper?" Mom said quickly.

"Yeah. They call it *papel picado*," Turk said. "I've been thinking about this thing since I came back from Mexico. This was the first chance I've had to do something about it."

She had done this, today. In what, an hour? Nobody could say my cousin wasn't a fast worker. Rude, and about as much fun as glass on your tongue, but she was good at what she did.

There was a painting on the easel. It was the head and shoulders of *The Scream* repeated over and over in different sizes.

Ileana went over and studied it under the dim light.

"They want to move," she said.

"Like they want to get away from that snake, maybe," Justin said.

"They can't," Turk said. "No feet."

Her other paintings were lined up along one side of the attic. Ileana went over to study them and we all followed.

Basically, they were every kind of way you could think of to paint *The Scream* and two-headed snakes. Or they were blotches of turquoise and black smeared together to make—smears, I guess.

"Do you exhibit?" Ileana asked after she'd walked up and down the line several times.

"I've had some shows," Turk said.

"She's won some prizes," Mom said.

"I am not surprised," Ileana said. "You are a true artist."

"See what you mean about the fish, though," Justin said. "Wouldn't fit in in a place like this."

"I've been thinking about that," Turk said. "Angelfish are aggressive, aren't they?"

"Well, if you don't feed 'em the tubifex worms, they can start chasing other fish around the tank," Justin said. "They get hungry for protein."

"Perfect," Turk said. "If the deal's still on, I want two

big black ones. I'll put the tank over there and keep the light on at night."

"Uh, okay," Justin said. "Two big black ones it is."

He looked like he was afraid he was turning over a couple of children to an unfit foster mother. Or maybe a wicked witch. But Justin would never go back on a promise.

And then a weird thing happened. All of a sudden, Ileana and Turk started to have this long talk about art. It seemed long. (It didn't really go on more than ten minutes.) A lot of words tumbled into the room, like *chiaroscuro,* and *Fauvism,* and *Rothko*. And for those minutes, the rest of us weren't there.

And when they were over, Turk went over to her easel and pulled off the painting and handed it to Ileana.

"Here," she said. "You get it."

"I would not have asked," Ileana said. "But thank you. Will you sign it?"

Turk did, with a little sort of twist beside her name that I guess was supposed to be the snake.

Mom suggested coffee, and we all went back downstairs.

I kept waiting for my cousin to do something else insulting, like ask Ileana and Justin to fly around the room, but she didn't. In fact, I had the feeling that, somehow, up in that attic, she and Ileana had connected. Ileana loved anything that came from people's imaginations. And Turk had plenty of that.

So we finished the coffee and Ileana and Justin left, and Turk went back up to her belfry.

Mom followed her up there to try to talk her into accepting some pillows and blankets, since she wouldn't accept a normal room with furniture.

"That could have been so much worse," Dad said, and poured himself another glass of wine.

"Lucky us," I said.

Dad was right. Compared to what Turk was capable of in the trouble department, it hadn't gone badly. Now if I could just get through the next three years at Vlad Dracul.

5

There's a thing the jenti do that's called the Rustle. It's nothing you can really hear. But if you hang around them long enough, you can tell when it's happening. It's a way they have of telling each other something is changing. Asking, "Have you noticed?" and "What do you think about it?" without ever moving their lips. Jenti may act as though they couldn't care less what's going on, but they always know when something is.

And Turk was something to Rustle about. As soon as she pulled up in her little black Volksbug and parked in a slot that was big enough for a stretch limo, and the four of us got out, it started.

New kid, coming in with Ileana (the Princess) Antonescu,

and Cody (the Original Gadje) Elliot, and Justin (World's First Swimming Jenti) Warrener, and who does she think she is, one of us? And if she doesn't, what does she think she is?

It was a fair question. Turk had decked herself out in black leather, even though the day was hot, and from her ears and around her neck dangled shards of mirror that flashed and glittered every time she moved. She wore the jewel Ileana had given her hanging on her forehead, and on her neck she'd drawn two black dots and the words OPEN HERE.

Rustle, Rustle, Rustle.

"What's with all the cars?" Turk said. "Why don't they just fly to school?"

"There's an old law against flying inside the town limits," Justin said. "Goes back to before there were airplanes. Not really enforced anymore. Still, it's not done very much."

"If it were me, I'd fly everywhere," Turk said.

"A lot of folks would think you were showing off," Justin said.

"Damn right," Turk said. "I would be. Why not?"

"We jenti say, 'Gold hidden is gold kept,' " Ileana said.

"Gold's no good unless you spend it," Turk said.

Because Turk was brand-new, she had an appointment with Mr. Horvath, the principal, as soon as we hit the door.

"Maybe I should wait for her," I said to Ileana and Justin when she went in.

"Good idea," Justin said. "See you in English."

"And at dinner," Ileana said. Lunch at Vlad Dracul was always called dinner, and was laid out like a banquet.

The gong for first period sounded its low note through the halls, and the jenti disappeared into their classrooms.

I was left alone with the dim light, the marble walls, and the scent of cedar from the doors.

I had never thought it would feel like I belonged at Vlad, but I had to admit, that was exactly how it felt now. It would be too much to say that I was glad to be back. But it was familiar, and I knew I had a place here. A place I'd earned.

The sound of quick, heavy steps coming down the stairs made me look up.

Gregor Dimitru came down them like a tall, angry wolf, and brushed past me with a short nod.

I had a sort of touchy relationship with Gregor. He'd touched me on my first day at Vlad, when he'd started to beat me up. Then Ileana had marked me with her protection. Another touch. Then she and I had fallen for each other, and Gregor had felt frozen out, even though Ileana had never wanted him for a boyfriend, or for anything else. So he and I had spent last semester, up to the last day, basically hating each other. Right at the end, things had improved a little between us. I had no idea what to expect now.

"Hey, Gregor," I said.

He nodded and went past me into the office. I heard the door to Horvath's inner office open and close. A minute later, an odd sound came from behind it. It might have been a sort of strangled yelp. And it did not sound like my cousin had made it.

A second later, Turk and Gregor were standing beside me. Horvath was right behind them.

He smiled when he saw me. It was not a friendly smile.

"Master Cody," Mr. Horvath said. "Welcome—back." Horvath was not a member of the Cody Elliot Fan Club any more than Gregor was.

"Thanks," I said.

The door closed.

"Come with me, please," Gregor said to Turk.

"No wolf, so I get this guy to show me around," Turk said. "See you, Cuz."

I had my own classes to get to, but I couldn't leave without knowing what had happened in Horvath's office.

"What did you say to Horvath?" I whispered.

"Not much," Turk said. "He asked me what I was interested in. I said, 'Rage, despair, and vengeance.' Then he asked how I saw myself fitting in at Vlad Dracul. I said I didn't. He didn't seem to like that, so I said, 'It's cool. If I have to go to school for a few more months, I'd rather do it with a bunch of vampires than anybody else.'"

Gregor's pale skin turned dark.

"Listen, Turk. You have got to stop calling people vampires," I said. "It's rude."

"I don't care," Turk said.

"You should," I said.

"Oh, *should*. That's my favorite word," Turk said. "Know what *should* really means, cousin? It means 'I don't like what's happening now.' That's all."

"No it doesn't." I was practically speaking in a normal voice now. In the halls of Vlad, that's like shouting. "It means—it means—Look, your English teacher is Shadwell. He writes poetry and textbooks. Ask him what *should* really means."

"Gee, do you think I should?" Turk said.

"It is customary not to speak above a whisper in the halls," Gregor said.

We were at the top of the stairs, where most of the junior and senior classes were.

"This is the class of English," Gregor said. "You are to enter."

Gregor was from Europe, so sometimes his English got a little odd. Usually, this was not a good sign. It tended to go with his skin turning dark, and his beating people up.

They went in, and I went back downstairs. Gregor and Turk. If Horvath had wanted to put the two wrongest people at Vlad together, he couldn't have done better. It was like putting one of Justin's angelfish in with something else, a clown loach, maybe, and waiting for the fight to start.

I got through the first three periods without hearing that Turk had been expelled, or thrown out a window. I collected my first batch of impossible assignments in math, biology, and history. Ah, yes, history.

Mr. Gibbon, the same teacher I'd had last year, told us our semester grade would be based on the book, treatise, or dissertation we would write on a subject from New Sodom history. That was in addition to the readings we would do from *Hidden Heritage: The Jenti Presence in American History* and the essays we would write on what we read, and the thousand pages of outside reading we would have to do.

"The addition of New Sodom history to the curriculum of this class is an idea of mine," he said in the faraway voice he always used. "The topic of local history is endlessly fascinating in itself, of course. Moreover, what was once dismissed as mere antiquarianism has become a legitimate field of historical inquiry. And in the case of our unique community, it is, perhaps, especially intriguing. It is an area in which one may make original contributions to the study of the past, and I look forward to receiving yours."

Sometimes I wondered if Mr. Gibbon was boring on

purpose, or if it just came naturally to him, like his flaky skin and gaunt, bony face.

Then came dinner, a subject in which I was as good as anybody at Vlad. When I got to the dining hall, it was just the same as it had been last year, with white-coated waiters and silver trays. The only difference was there were no water polo jocks shouting and throwing food.

Ileana and Justin were already at a table. They had saved places for me and Turk.

"How's it going so far?" Justin asked me.

"Same as last year. Impossible," I said. "I have to write a book or something on New Sodom history. Sheesh. I don't know anything about this place that you didn't tell me."

"Well, there's a lot to know," Justin said. "Pretty interesting, some of it."

"Yeah, but a whole book," I said. "What's that, seventy thousand, a hundred thousand words?"

"More or less," Justin said. "Maybe you ought to do a play. Plays average twenty thousand."

"Maybe a musical," I said. "Except that I hate musicals."

"I could sing in it," Ileana said. "I will be taking a class in vocal music."

Justin's mom, who had been teaching Ileana piano for years, had a new part-time job teaching a couple of classes in the music department.

"Musical history," I said. "I could tell Gibbon it was a new form."

Turk came into the dining hall. I beckoned her over.

"I thought this place was going to be hard," she said as she sat down.

"What did Shadwell say about *should*?" I asked her.

"He said it was an interesting insight, and everybody should write an essay on it. Five thousand words." She stretched and said, "If I can just keep awake, I'll do okay here."

"So, you like it okay, then?" Justin asked.

"Too posh," Turk said. "Way too posh. But apart from that, what's there not to like?"

"Well, some people think the work is kind of hard," Justin said.

Turk shrugged.

"Not so far," she said.

"It is good that you feel so confident," Ileana said.

"Where's Gregor?" I asked.

"I told him to get lost," Turk said. "How hard is it to find your way down a hallway? Besides, he's a jerk. That phony accent."

"It's not phony," I said. "He talks that way. He's from Europe."

"Some kind of exchange student?" Turk said.

"There are dormitories for students from overseas," Ileana explained. "Jenti from all over the world come to Vlad."

Gregor came in at that point. He was with his friends Ilie, Constantin, and Vladimir. They sat down together and bent their heads toward him. Gregor was angry about something, and I had a pretty good idea, in a general way, what it was.

One of the waiters hurried over to their table.

"What's up with that? That waiter acts like he's afraid of him," Turk said.

"Not afraid," Justin said. "Gregor's pretty high jenti. Some folks don't mind showing him they know it."

38

"Jerk," Turk said.

Then Gregor stood up and stalked over to our table.

I tensed, figuring our on-again-off-again acquaintance-ship was off again, but he wasn't coming to see me.

"You spoke something in world history third period," he said to Turk.

"Yep," Turk said.

"What did you mean when Mr. Von Ranke asked, 'What is the essence of the jenti situation in the world?' and you said, 'Ingratitude'?"

"I thought it was pretty clear," Turk said. "*Ingratitude* means—"

"I know what it means," Gregor said. "What I am really asking is, how dare you say such a thing, when you know nothing of us?"

"Do you remember who talked before I did?" Turk asked.

"Yes. It was I," Gregor said.

"Mm-hm. You went on for five minutes about how the vampires have always been persecuted, and everybody was nodding along with you. And it just sounded like you didn't have a clue in your head about where *you* are."

"What do you mean?" Gregor said.

"I mean, look around you," Turk said. "For God's sake, man, half the world goes to bed hungry at night. And what's your biggest problem? Yours, personally."

"You have no right to say anything about us," Gregor said.

"What is *your* problem, man? *Your* biggest problem?" Turk went on.

"Do not try to reduce this to a question of myself," Gregor said. "That is not the point."

"It's my point," Turk said. "You've got everything, for God's sake. You wouldn't know real trouble if it pantsed you, tied you up, and left you in a tree house."

For a second, Gregor looked puzzled. As insults went, that was a left-fielder. And the image was so ridiculous that I think he might have laughed.

Except I beat him to it. I couldn't help it.

And that made Gregor turn on me.

"Sorry, man," I said, trying to apologize. "She did that to me once. Except for the pants part."

Justin put his hand over his eyes.

Ileana dropped hers.

Because one thing you did not ever want to do with Gregor was to attack his dignity, and he clearly had decided that we had just done that.

And there was one other thing that everybody at the table knew but Turk. It was the answer to her question to Gregor. Gregor didn't have Ileana. I did. And he still hadn't gotten over that.

Gregor stood there twitching, with his pale skin turning dark red. No one had ever actually seen Gregor lose it. There was always this iciness about his anger, even when he was beating you up. But now he looked like his head might pop off the top of his neck.

"You are ignorant. Useless. Arrogant. Even your stupid cousin is better than you," he finally said to Turk. He stumbled over the words, which was not like Gregor. He usually said something fang-sharp and sarcastic when he was mad.

"But not wrong," Turk said slowly.

Ileana reached over and put her hand on Gregor's arm. She flicked her eyes.

Gregor looked around and saw that everyone in the dining hall was watching our table.

"You will never know how wrong you are," Gregor said.

"Ooh. Slash," Turk said, drawing one of her long black nails along her throat.

Gregor shook his arm free, snarled in a way that made me think what a great wolf he probably made, and turned away.

"Oh, boy," I thought. "Welcome to tenth grade. Thank you, Turk."

Turk turned back to her food.

"You know," she said, "this salmon mousse is really good."

But Ileana wasn't going to let her change the subject that easily.

"You have a point, Turquoise," she said. "But not as strong a point as you think. You have judged him too quickly. And Gregor has a point, too, don't you think?"

"What I think is that he's a spoiled, whiney brat," Turk said.

"Gregor would not tell you this, but his mother is dead," Ileana said. "Is that, perhaps, a large enough personal problem for you to respect?"

"Let me tell you something, Ileana," Turk said. "About why I don't worry whether I'm rude or not. It's because people are always rude to me. And why? Because I don't look like them. Don't think like them. Don't want to be like them. I don't insult them just because they're all about rock stars, or jock stars, or video games. I don't care about that stuff, but I don't dump on the people who do. But if you look like me, if you act a little different from what they're used to, they'll circle around you and try to peck out your eyes. And I'll tell you something else. These vampire friends of yours don't know how lucky they are. A whole school of people exactly like themselves to hang out with. A whole school. And I can't even find one person."

She got up from the table and left.

It was going to be a long year.

6

By the end of the day, the Rustle had gotten louder.

The new one. The cousin. She and Gregor are fighting. She was rude to him. Rude to our princess.

It was around me in gym, where we played half-court basketball, and I thought I heard it in the squeaks and whispers of the sneakers. It was in the scrape of Mr. Gibbon's chalk on the blackboard during history. And by the time I walked into my last class, it was almost loud enough to actually hear. In fact, I did hear it. It was silence. Absolute and perfect silence.

"Welcome, Master Cody," said the teacher, Ms. Magyar. "Or should I say—" And she rattled off some syllables that sounded like water running over stones. A greeting in high jenti that meant "Come before me bringing the joy of your presence." It was one of about six high jenti phrases I knew. High jenti was so elaborate and formal that almost nobody spoke it anymore. Jenti kids in New Sodom spoke a lingo of jenti, English, and a few other languages. There were no rules, and it was always changing. But I knew one jenti girl who did know the old language, because she had to. And I was going to learn it for her. It was a surprise. I hadn't told Ileana or anyone I was taking this class. And no other gadje ever had.

Anyway, I said the same thing back to Ms. Magyar, and the room cracked up. I mean, cracked up jenti style. All of the heads that had been turned my way looked down at their desks, and seven pairs of shoulders went up like they were trying to flap.

"The proper response is—" Ms. Magyar said, and made some sounds like gears grinding. "The approximate translation in English would be 'I fly toward the bright moon of your splendor.'"

"Thank you," I said in one of the other high jenti things I knew. It really meant, "Your gift is beyond the deserving, O radiant friend."

But Ms. Magyar giggled. "That was creditable, Master Cody. But as you spoke the words, they meant, 'Your gift is beyond the nothing, O radiant horse.'"

The shoulder blades were twitching like mad.

By the time class was over, I knew that in high jenti there were twenty-seven words for groups of men, and twenty-nine for groups of women. Nouns inflected, whatever that was, to fourteen cases, whatever they were. There were three alternative conjugations for most verbs, and a thing could be male, female, or neuter depending on which of the conjugations you were using.

It was going to be lots of fun.

But not as much fun as my fourth-period class had been. English class. One thousand pages of outside reading per semester, and of course *Some Further Glories of English Literature* by Norman P. Shadwell. Apart from that, just the odd essay, sonnet cycle, or novella.

The last gong chimed through the halls. Feeling slightly as though I'd been run over by a truck, I went down to Ileana's chorus class.

They must have been running late. The door was still closed. Through it came a sad old song sung in high jenti. Even though I didn't understand a word, I felt the sorrow. And the singer, whoever he was, was fantastic. It was a powerful voice, kind of deep, and rich. Some of the singers in the old movies my parents liked to watch were like that. Not my kind of thing, but I knew it was good.

The song stopped.

The door opened.

I looked in.

Gregor was standing next to Mrs. Warrener's piano, looking over her shoulder at some sheet music.

"Thank you, Gregor," she said. She said it in that old New England way that means a lot more than the words.

Wow. Gregor. I'd have sooner expected him to have a hidden talent for being nice.

The jenti were impressed, too. You could tell. Their eyes were shining.

He looked my way and I wanted to say something, and I wanted it to be special. So I said, "Your gift is beyond the deserving, O radiant friend."

The whole class turned their eyes on me.

Rustle, Rustle. *The gadje friend is learning high jenti. What a good friend he is.* Rustle.

So I had snitched Gregor's moment of glory. Swell.

He didn't say anything, just got his stuff and went past me.

"All I wanted to do was be nice," I said to Ileana.

"You were. You are. Some people are hard to be nice to," Ileana said.

And up came the other person I knew who fit that description, right on cue.

"I haven't been this bored since the last time Mom got married," Turk said. "I thought a school full of vampires would be exciting. This place is about as interesting as a cemetery."

I didn't say anything. I just wished the French Foreign Legion took girls.

"Shall we visit the student center?" Ileana smiled. "Perhaps you would like that."

"Whatever," Turk said.

The center was the way it always was after school: quiet and elegant and full of whispering jenti.

Turk looked around at the oak-paneled walls and the oil paintings that hung on them and said, "You could get a really great headbanger concert going in here. Anybody ever done it?"

"Sure," I said. "The same day we had the pig fights. It was real popular."

Turk just shook her head. "I can't handle this place. I need some grunge."

And she left.

"Perhaps we should go with her," Ileana said. "She does not know New Sodom well. She might become lost."

"I was sort of hoping," I said.

"She is your family, Cody," Ileana said. "You must help her. She is in great pain."

"She is a great pain," I said.

"Stop it," Ileana said, and led me out of the center.

We caught up to Turk in the parking lot.

"You don't have to come with me," she said, and drove off. Her little black car sounded like it was cursing us.

"Do I still have to be nice to her?" I said.

"Yes," Ileana said. "And so do I. But we do not have to like it."

Getting home was no problem. There were stretch limos for anybody who wanted them, or Ileana could call for her own car and have it there in minutes.

But she said, "Let us walk home today. To my house. You will get a ride from there."

The way to Ileana's house led down quiet streets shaded by fine old trees whose leaves were just beginning to turn gold at their tips.

I took Ileana's hand.

"It will all be well," she said.

"You really think so?" I said.

"Yes," Ileana said. "Turk is vain and silly, but she is not stupid. She will find something hard to do, and she will do it, and then she will think less about herself and more about whatever that thing is. She has a large soul, and she needs to feed it."

She looked up at me and smiled a wicked little smile.

"She is rather a lot like you, you know."

"No way," I said. "I'm not that bad."

"Not now," she said. "But when you came, you were very full of the act you were putting on. But then you found your big thing. You decided to challenge us to admit that you could be as good as we thought we were. And you did, and you are."

I looked at Ileana and thought about how smart she was. No, not smart. Wise. Wise in a very special way that I would probably never really understand.

Then I did something very brave. I said what I said next. Which was "I found something bigger than that. I found you."

And I kissed her under the trees.

I don't know how long we stood there. A week or two, maybe. But when we broke, she said, "This was why I wanted to walk home."

"We'll never make it at this rate," I said.

And we kissed again.

Eventually, we made it up the long hill to Ileana's house. And Ileana had her limo take me home.

"All will be well," she said again, as the car pulled away from the curb.

I wished right then that I were old enough to drive. It was a comedown to walk my girlfriend home kissing her and then be hauled away by somebody else, like a little kid. But overall, I thought, things were pretty good just then.

7

There was no little black car sitting in front of the house when I got home.

"Where's Turk?" Mom said as I came in the door.

"She took off by herself after school," I said. "For all I know, she's on her way back to Mexico."

"Did she have a bad day at school?" Mom asked.

"She gave about as good as she got," I said.

"What does that mean, exactly?" Mom asked. She wasn't happy.

"It means she insulted everyone she could, sneered at everything except lunch, and felt sorry for herself all day," I said. "You know. She was Turk."

"Cody, I really wish you'd be more supportive right

now," Mom snapped. "This is very difficult for all of us. I know Turk isn't the easiest person in the world to be around, but she needs help."

"She doesn't want help," I said. "If she'd been on the *Titanic,* she'd have jumped into the water and bragged about how cool she was."

"That's not helpful," Mom said.

"It's not supposed to be," I said. "Look, can we fight about how mean I am some other time? I have a lot of homework."

Mom waved me away.

I went up the stairs, stomping on every one. Turk. Damn Turk. Even when she wasn't around, she caused trouble. Mom and I never fought. That was a Dad and me thing.

I slammed the door to my room, threw my backpack on the floor, and talked to the ceiling until it was time to eat.

Turk didn't come home for dinner. The long sunset left the sky, and a few stars came out. Still no Turk. Dad tried calling her cell phone, but no answer.

Finally, long after midnight, her little car grumbled up in front of the house and she slammed through the front door and up the stairs to her attic.

By the time the three of us got up and into the hall, the ladder was up.

"Turk, come down now. We need to talk," Dad shouted.

Then we watched as the little rope that pulled down the ladder disappeared up through its hole.

"Turk!" Dad said.

Then Mom put her hand on his arm.

"That's just what she wants you to do," she said. "Let's go back to bed. We'll deal with this tomorrow when we're all rested. And when she can't turn it into a drama."

"Good thinking," Dad said. "Cody, back to bed."

"Right, Dad," I said. "No drama."

Saying "No drama" and "Turk" in the same sentence was like saying "No homework" and "Vlad." But I knew Dad would like the sound of it.

I went to bed. Down the hall, I heard my mom and dad doing the same thing. A few low whispers. Lights out.

Then I lay there wondering what Turk had been up to.

For the first time, I wondered how someone who wanted to knock on Turk's door would do it.

And would Turk answer? She had to be enjoying a good mad right now. Ignoring me would give her extra pleasure.

I stared up at the ceiling for a couple of minutes. Then I had an idea that I thought would work.

I tiptoed into the hall carrying the chair from my desk like it would explode if I dropped it. I stood on it and scratched my nails slowly over the trapdoor. Slowly. Quietly. For a long time.

Finally, the hatch cracked open.

"You're doing that wrong," Turk said in a whisper.

"Of course," I agreed.

"You're only supposed to use your little finger. Using your whole hand is rude," Turk said.

"I'll never do it again," I said.

"Anyway, what do you want?" Turk said.

"Just wanted to talk," I said. "Let down the ladder."

"I can't," Turk said. "Your parents will wake up."

"It's okay. They aren't going to kill you tonight," I said.

Slowly, Turk pushed down the ladder. The springs skreaked, but the door to Mom and Dad's room stayed closed.

"Come on up," Turk said.

The attic looked like it was forty fathoms underwater. The only light came from the ten-gallon fish tank that Justin had given her. Two black angelfish darted back and forth in it, expecting to be fed. Pale green light and black shadows shimmered on the walls. The Snake of Life over our heads was like some half-seen monster, and *The Scream* standing in the corner looked like a drowning victim. Turk had really made the place her own.

"What do you know about Crossfield?" she asked me.

"Crossfield? What were you doing in Crossfield?" I asked.

"Just looking around," Turk said.

"That's not a good place for looking around," I said. "Especially after dark."

I had been to Crossfield once. Dad had made a wrong turn shortly after we'd moved to New Sodom, and we'd ended up there. From what I had seen then, and from what I had learned about the place since, I hadn't seen any reason to go back. Apart from the factories and a few other buildings that might have been houses once, the place was mostly empty lots full of concrete and rusted iron, strange-looking weeds, abandoned cars stripped of their wheels and engines. And under it all you could still see little cobblestoned roads lacing back and forth, running at right angles.

"It's a great place for looking around," Turk said. "So ugly it's beautiful."

"So ugly it's ugly," I said.

"The moon drowning in that dirty river," Turk said. "Buildings like skulls everywhere, staring at you."

"By which I assume you mean the abandoned mills," I said.

"Is that what they are?" Turk said. "Really abandoned?"

"Mills and factories," I said.

"I want one," Turk said.

"No problem," I said. "Would you like fries with that?"

"I need space," Turk said. "I need a real studio. In real towns, places like that would have been converted years ago. Hey, in some places, they give artists tax breaks to move in. Those things are just sitting there. Waiting. Waiting for me. Your dad's got to help me find out who owns those places and how I can get into one."

"So you want Dad to buy you an abandoned mill so you can have a place to paint?" I said.

"And sculpt," Turk said.

"Great idea," I said. "At last you'd have enough space for your whole ego."

"Listen, jerk," Turk said. "Do you know why cities turn buildings like that over to artists? Money. Money follows art around like a lost puppy. Even Uncle Jack can understand that. I'll cut him in."

"Good idea," I said. "Dad's always wanted to be part-owner of an abandoned building with a wannabe painter in it."

"I am not a damn wannabe," Turk snarled. "I produce. I sell."

"Good night, Turk," I said. "Good luck with Dad."

I went back down the ladder.

I heard it thump up behind me.

I had to admit, I was glad Turk was home safe. But what kind of nut job cousin did I have?

"Buy me a mill, Uncle Jack. I want to paint my pictures there." It was like she was still making spaceships out of cardboard.

But as I got into bed, I thought that maybe Crossfield

could be the topic of my impossible research paper for Gibbon's history class. It wasn't a blinding flash of inspiration. I wasn't even very interested in it. But Turk was sort of right about the place. It hadn't been beautiful, but it had been intriguing in a twisted kind of way. Like a car wreck. There might be a story there.

8

Mom, Dad, and I were sitting around the breakfast table the next morning. We looked just like one of those paintings of happy families you see on old magazine covers, except that we didn't look happy. Dad was scowling, and Mom's lips were a thin line in her face.

Turk slouched into the room, poured a cup of coffee, grabbed my toast out of my hand, stuffed it into her mouth, and swallowed it with the coffee.

"Thanks," she said.

"You're welcome," I said. "Good morning, Turk. It's nice to see you. Are you all ready for school?"

"Turk, we were very worried about you last night," Mom said. "We had no idea where you were, or if you were

55

all right. You could at least have called. Please don't do that again."

"I didn't have anything to say last night," Turk said. "But I do now. Uncle Jack, I need some space of my own. Like one of those old mills in Crossfield."

"What is this with Crossfield?" Dad said.

"It's the next big thing," I said. "Urban decay. Better catch the wave while you can, Dad."

"Cody!" Dad said. "Anyway, Turk, do I understand you correctly? Are you asking me to buy you an abandoned mill?"

"Yeah," said Turk. "I know just the one I want."

"Oh," said Dad. "Good. Just wanted to be sure. No. I will not buy you an abandoned mill."

"I knew it," Turk said, and slammed out of the kitchen. She got into her car and peeled away from the curb, leaving me to wait for the school limo.

I relaxed in the car with the usual morning crew: Anton, Istvan, Janos, Anastaizia, Gizi, and Trescka. They were the same kids who'd snubbed me last year, walling me out behind their special language. Now things were different.

"Come and rest beneath the shadow of our wings, O radiant horse," Gizi said, and giggled.

"Your horse is beyond deserving," I said.

And then we all switched to English.

New Sodom went past the windows slowly, and it was another beautiful day, the morning sun bright on the houses and the shadows extra dark under the trees.

It was perfect—the weather, the quiet car, the jenti chatting softly about little things with each other and with me.

So I said, "Hey, anybody know the story on Crossfield?"

And the chatting stopped and the car was real, real quiet.

Finally, Istvan said, "No."

And Anton said, "Not really."

And Janos shrugged.

And Anastaizia, Gizi, and Trescka looked out the windows.

When we got to school, everyone hurried off and left me except Gizi, who said, "Some things . . . ," and shook her head.

Which was clearly all the explanation I was going to get.

Now I was really curious. And when I was curious about anything jenti, I could always ask Justin for a straight answer.

But Justin and I didn't have classes together in the morning. And it wasn't until dinner that we saw each other.

Ileana was with us, and there was an empty seat. Turk had started sitting at a table by herself. She was across the room, writing in a black notebook and shoving her food into her face without looking at it.

"Listen," I said. "Turk visited Crossfield last night."

No reaction from Ileana.

Justin said, "Oh."

"So anyway, she came home with this weird idea that my dad should buy her one of the old mills and let her turn it into a studio. The whole thing."

"Hm," Justin said.

Ileana put down her fork.

"But then I got to thinking—why doesn't anybody talk about Crossfield, or go there? And why is it just a ruin? It doesn't make sense."

I waited for an answer.

Justin pushed something around on his plate. Ileana didn't do anything.

Finally, she said, "This is not a good place to talk about it."

"Oh," I said. If Justin had said that, I would have said, "Okay, where can we go to talk?" But the way Ileana said it sounded like there was no good place on earth to answer my question.

"I've been thinking I might do my local history project on it," I said.

"Bad idea," Justin said.

"Why?" I said.

"Excuse us, please, Cody," Justin said.

And that was the end of our conversation. He and Ileana got up and walked out of the dining hall.

It looked like if I ever wanted complete privacy at Vlad, all I had to do was say the word *Crossfield* and I'd get it.

What was there about Crossfield that was so awful that Ileana and Justin would both walk out on me? Some weird New Sodom secret that everybody knew and nobody talked about?

I had one more idea. And after my last class, I went to the library.

Ms. Shadwell, the librarian, greeted me like she was a starving wolf and I was a sandwich. Since Ms. Shadwell was one of those jenti who turn into a wolf at times, this made me a little nervous. Actually, Ms. Shadwell always made me a little nervous. She wasn't much like your usual librarian.

"Master Cody," she practically roared. "It's so nice to see

you again. Did you have a good summer? I've got some great new books I've just finished cataloging. Let me show them to you. Do you like fantasy? I forget. Anyway, we've got that new trilogy everyone's talking about. Oh, and I have some new histories. Do you like the Civil War? Oh, and there's this fascinating book on diesel engines if you like those—"

"Actually, I am here about history," I said. "I have that project on New Sodom to write this year."

"Excellent," she said, like I'd given her a present. "We have everything on New Sodom. Population stats, public records, newspapers, ephemera—would you like to see my ephemera collection?"

"What would that be, exactly?" I asked.

"Oh, ephemera are so much fun," she chortled. "All kinds of things. Posters, notices, little commemorative booklets and souvenirs. I have broadsides that go back to the sixteen hundreds advertising anvils for sale. Lots of wonderful things."

"I've been thinking about writing about Crossfield," I said.

Ms. Shadwell stopped chortling. I saw the wolf come into her eyes.

"Oh, I'm afraid there's nothing," she said. "That place wasn't regarded as local."

"But it's part of the town, isn't it?"

"Well, I suppose you might say that it is now," she said. "But it wasn't originally. So I'm afraid there's nothing. We do have a nice collection of sewer maps."

"Well, maybe I could take a look at those ephemera, then," I said. I thought it might be a good idea to pretend to be interested in something. And the ephemera, whatever they were, had to be better than sewer maps.

"Excellent," Ms. Shadwell said, happy again.

She took me across the room to a big wooden door and unlocked it. A sign over the door said SPECIAL COLLECTIONS.

On the other side of the door was a room that looked like it had been built to store nightmares. High, long, narrow, and dark, with a single table running from the door almost to the back wall, it was filled with shelves that ran to the ceiling and were crammed with books bound in black leather. A tall ladder on rails ran to the ceiling. There were little lights with green glass shades spaced regularly down the table's length, and along the table were two long benches, one on each side. A chill rose from the dark slate floor. There was one window high up, which looked like it had been meant for shooting arrows through. No light from it reached the floor.

"It's so good you're getting an early start on your project," Ms. Shadwell said. "You can have the entire room to yourself today. Later in the year there'll be students at every one of these lights. Now let's find those ephemera."

She took me all the way down to the end of the room and pulled two huge volumes off the shelves. She held them as if they were as light as a couple of paperbacks.

"These are the seventeenth and eighteenth centuries," she said. "Of course, there's a great deal more in the nineteenth. Three volumes, in fact. And the twentieth—well, I still haven't got all that cataloged. And the 1950s are at the bindery in Boston. Seven volumes. But they'll be back soon if you want to see them. But why don't you start here and see if anything piques your interest? Would you like to see those anvil advertisements?"

"Well, sure," I said.

Ms. Shadwell left me with my own pair of white gloves from a box in the room and went out.

"I'll be back when we close," she said as she left. "I'm afraid I have to lock you in. Most of these things are irreplaceable."

"Me too," I said. "So please don't forget I'm in here."

She laughed and locked the door.

I turned on one of the table lamps. It had been specially designed to give as little light as possible. A small circle of pale yellow fell onto the dark wood. The rest of the room was almost totally black. Turk would have loved it.

I didn't. So I went around the table and turned on every one of the lights. That was better. Now the dark spines of the books glinted where their gold titles hadn't faded, and the table shone. It was almost comfortable.

I flipped open one of the books Ms. Shadwell had given me.

"*At sale A Fine Milch Cow of Three Years,*" said the page I opened to. "*Two Pounds Sterling.*"

I tried another.

"*A Substitute for Militia Duty is Defired. Twenty fhillings for fix weeks' Service. Apply to William Fletcher at the Fletcher Farm.*"

I could see why Ms. Shadwell was so interested in these things. The suspense was killing me.

I looked around the room at all those closed black books, filled with things the jenti had saved from their long years in New Sodom. I felt like they were smirking at me.

"Think you know our secrets, gadje? Think we'll tell you about anything that really matters?"

Ms. Shadwell had put me in here to overwhelm me with this stuff, but that didn't mean I had to be overwhelmed. She'd be back in an hour and a half to let me out. Meanwhile, I was going to play on the ladder.

I climbed up to the top and pushed myself around the room as fast as I could. That wasn't very fast, but at the top of a twelve-foot ladder it felt a little scary. I reached the opposite side of the room and did it again, from the middle rungs this time. Not as much fun.

Then I had another idea. I would pile all the books I could onto the table and leave them for Ms. Shadwell. One good overwhelming deserved another.

"Gee, Ms. Shadwell, it's all so interesting I couldn't decide where to start." That's what I'd say.

So I started unloading the shelves. Up and down the ladder, just pulling stuff off at random until I had an armload, then setting it carefully on the table, making higher and higher stacks. Pretty soon, I had something that looked like the skyline of a fairly big city. But all the buildings looked the same, except for their heights. I wanted some variety. So I started scouting through the shelves for the smallest books I could find, making little pyramids on top of my favorite skyscrapers.

I named the tallest one the Ileana Tower. Another was the Warrener Building. And there was the Elliot State Building.

I checked my watch. Forty-five minutes to go.

Small books, small books.

I found *The Ploughman's Guide to Successful Corn Husbandry, A Brief Treatise on the Metallurgy of Copper, Proceedings of the New Sodom Reform Society, 1845.* Great stuff for the tops of buildings.

And I found *The Journal of Mercy Warrener*.

If its spine had ever had gold letters, they were long gone. The covers were worn and brown, not black. And inside, the paper was of different kinds. Some was as fine as the pages of a really good Bible. Some was yellow, and crackled when I touched it. Some was rough-edged and smaller than the rest. All of it had been written on in a strange, beautiful hand that swooped across the page in a way I'd never seen.

I wondered if Mercy Warrener had been an ancestor of Justin's. That would make this journal a lot more interesting. And it was possible. In some jenti families, the husband took the wife's name, if the family was important. Ileana's family was like that. But then, they were royalty. As far as I knew, the Warreners were just old New Sodom.

I flipped the book open and read this:

February 18, 1676

The men came and took Father. He fought mightily, but they were too many. They have taken him to Crossfield. Mother and Prudence and the baby and I were all hid in the secret place which Father did make for us against this day. They made to burn our house, and so find us out, but Captain Danforth came with his men and did prevent them. Two of the enemy were slain and drunk from, but the rest were safe in Crossfield.

All this we were told when Captain Danforth, who knew where we were, did come to us and convey us to this place of safety. We see the fires now against the night, and know that our house must be one of them. Captain Danforth says we shall take the town again, but our men are so few, and the militias from Boston and the towns around it do make the enemy stronger by the hour.

If my Beloved were here, I believe that this never would have happened. He and Father together might have stood off the whole company of gadje until Captain Danforth and his men appeared under their double-headed eagle. But he is far away and will not return to me.

Mother do hold the baby and rock, humming a song that is not a song. I fear she may be mad, or near it. Prudence asks where Father be, and when he do be coming. I know, but cannot tell it. I cannot speak a word. My tongue be stone. But I write this, that this night may never be forgot.

When Ms. Shadwell came back, I didn't hear the door open. I was a long way away, with Mercy Warrener.

9

Ephemera. Bits of paper that don't have any permanent meaning. Bits of paper that survive a hundred years, two hundred years, three hundred years, and suddenly become important because they have survived.

That's what Mercy Warrener's journal was. Ephemera. But she had tried to give it meaning across the years.

The first page said:

> *I, Mercy Warrener, do leave this book for a remembrance to my family. These journals I have kept since I was a girl. Now, as I see the end of life approaching at last, these memories of the old times may serve to instruct and warn those whom I love so much. May God*

forgive any vain design I have in doing so. In my heart
I wish only to leave a token of the life of our family to
our family. May it continue in spite of all that has hap-
pened, and all that is to come.
    Mercy Warrener, 1818

The journal was really just a collection of odds and ends from Mercy Warrener's long life. Her personal ephemera. Most of what she had left behind was just the kind of thing that anybody might write about daily life. Of course, this was a daily life that had begun in 1650 and ended in 1820, which was kind of unusual, but nearly everything she had written was stuff like:

March 14, 1664
    A warm day and so we did wash the clothes after this long winter. They made a mound as high as the eaves of the house. We do all be very tired from the work. The blueberries will not soon be ripe to pick.

The next page was a recipe for robin pie.

But every once in a while, in the earliest entries, there would be a note at the bottom of whatever she was writing about.

    Thomas Thornton taken to Crossfield.
    Allen Ames taken to Crossfield.
    Hope Carlton taken to Crossfield.

These were names I knew. Names of the selkie kids on the water polo team. Friends. These were their ancestors, and it wasn't hard to figure out what "taken to Crossfield" probably meant.

Those entries stopped after 1676. That was when the Compact of New Sodom had been signed. From then on, the jenti families had done their drinking outside the town limits, and the gadje had left them in peace. That was something I'd learned from Justin. So nobody was taken to Crossfield after that.

But Mercy Warrener had lived through a lot of history besides the local battles between her people and the gadje. Once in a while, it had touched her.

April 20, 1775

There is great stir and doing. The militia have gone to join the army besieging Boston. The British did try to seize the stores of powder and shot at Concord, and have been sent back beaten by our men. I knew nothing of this until today, for I have been ill with the flux, and had my own war a-raging in my innards. Better today.

It is a terrible thing to be at war again, but this time all the folk of New Sodom do be of one heart. Our company be divided into one platoon of them and one of us. We hope they may do much good, and come home soon.

Then she had something about buying a calf and naming her Rose. But then came:

May 1, 1775

The flag I have been charged with making for the militia company be finished. I think it most handsome and fitting. No more will we see the Angel of New

Sodom of the gadje nor the silver eagle of the Mercians. They be put away, it may be forever. One new flag for all. There be two rattlesnakes twined together about an Angel of Liberty and the words "Don't Tread On Me" about them, all on a field of red. At the top of our banner in gold letters I have worked "New Sodom Combined Militia Company."

I had thought to put the words "Death to Tyrants" or "An Appeal to Heaven" about the snakes instead of what I have writ. It was young Nathan who did persuade me otherwise.

"Ancestress," he did say. "They are fine-looking snakes ye have made and I tell ye, 'Don't Tread On Me' is good advice and the Britishers should take it."

"I will do as you ask, descendant," I told him, "if ye will promise me to hunt no more rattlesnakes, but just to kill the ones that God may send ye." For he is fond of killing rattlesnakes and takes great pride in being called colonel though he is yet not thirteen.

"All right, then, ancestress," Nathan did say. "But only if ye will let me go to Boston with ye when ye present the new flag."

There was nothing in the journal about whether Nathan the rattlesnake killer (and colonel—what was that about?) had gone along to deliver the flag or not. But in April 1776 there was this:

April 18, 1776
The Company are home today. They came marching back from our freed Boston following the flag I had

made for them. Captain Mathers did let Nathan carry it into the town hall, where it is to hang until wanted again. God grant that be not soon, but Captain Mathers believes the war is not over yet.

Fife and drum played "Yankee Doodle." 'Tis a song I have never liked. An Englishman wrote it some years back to mock our militia. But now our men have taken it and made it ours. The joke is on the English, for they are fled from Boston and Massachusetts is free of them. Now I do love that song.

It was wonderful in my eyes to see our two folk marching home in ranks, one people under the flag I had made. It is the first time ever that we have truly been as one. It is my heart's wish that we may remain so. I do wish that there were some place where all of New Sodom might gather to share songs and stories and where the women might work quilts and the men carve furniture or do other work of the hands together. Then we might always be bonded, in peace as well as war. But I fear that, old as I am, I shall not live to see it.

And she hadn't. And she didn't ever mention it again. But I had the feeling it was on her mind from time to time. She wrote with such pleasure about doing things with her hands. She was so proud of Nathan for his beautiful singing voice. I was sure that her idea of bringing New Sodom together for what she called "play parties and work" had come back to her over and over.

And, by the end of that afternoon, I knew Mercy Warrener's mind better than anyone had in almost two hundred years. You couldn't not know somebody when they told you so much about the odds and ends of their life. When you have somebody's recipe for robin pie, and how many children they had, and the names of their cows, they become real to you in a way. I could hear her flat, soft voice, like Justin's but higher. I imagined her small, brown-haired, quiet, and strong, wearing a simple gray dress, and wooden shoes for working in her yard. It was like she was whispering in my ear.

There was another thing: Mercy Warrener had a broken heart. Every February 13 there would be the same note:

___ yeares since my Beloved did fly from me. And the wound be yet as fresh as the day he left.

Never anything else. Never any mention of the Beloved except for the one back in 1676. I wanted to know who that guy was. To go wherever he'd gone and tell him to get his fanged self back to New Sodom and the woman who loved him.

The key rattled in the lock. Ms. Shadwell came in and saw what I had done with the books.

"Goodness, Master Cody, you *have* developed an interest," she said.

Oops. Time for plan B. I didn't want Ms. Shadwell to know what Mercy had told me about Crossfield. I had a feeling that, if Ms. Shadwell knew what I had come across, it wouldn't be here the next time I wanted it.

"Let me help you put these back," I said, sliding Mercy's journal onto one of the stacks.

I put the book on the shelf where I'd found it, but I hid

it at the back, behind all three volumes of *Flora and Fauna of Gomorrah County, Massachusetts.*

"I hope you found something to get you started," Ms. Shadwell said from the top of the ladder.

"I might have," I said. "Do you know what a rattlesnake colonel was?"

Ms. Shadwell laughed.

"Oh, yes. Back in colonial times rattlesnakes were quite a problem around here. And the settlers were terrified of them. There was nothing like them in England. Hardly any poison snakes at all there. Certainly nothing that lets you know it's about to bite you. So the colonial assembly—"

"The General Court," I chirped.

"The General Court," Ms. Shadwell said. "The General Court passed a law that anyone who killed a rattlesnake could call himself colonel if he wanted to. It got to be quite a joke to call someone a rattlesnake colonel."

"Even if someone was just a kid?" I asked.

"Oh, yes. That was part of the joke. We had one young fellow in town, Nathan Warrener. He loved to hunt rattle-snakes. Took to calling himself colonel when he was younger than you. Folks laughed, but he didn't care. He ended up with more than a hundred rattlesnake skins. You might ask Master Justin to show you the skins sometime. Last I heard, the family still had the collection."

You know how it is when you find out something new and you can't stop thinking about it? That's how it was with me and Mercy Warrener. It was almost like being a little kid and having an imaginary friend. But the thing was, Mercy Warrener hadn't been imaginary. She had lived where I lived. Her descendant was my best friend. So when I went home that afternoon, it was almost like I had two sets of eyes. I saw everything twice.

"Those are cars, Mercy," I said in my head. "That big thing's a bus. The trees on this street are awful old. Did you see them when they were young, or was this part of town not built yet? That's First Congregational over there. I know you went there. Not the building you remember, though, right?"

Dad noticed at dinner I wasn't my usual charming self.

"Is everything all right, Cody?" he asked. "You're being quiet."

"Well," I said, "I'm thinking about this woman I sort of met today. A relative of Justin's."

"Oh, ho. Does Ms. Antonescu have a rival, then?" Dad said.

"Not exactly," I said. "She died in 1820."

"Then I predict this relationship will go nowhere," Dad said.

"Hah," I said. "Very funny." And went on thinking about Mercy Warrener.

As it would turn out, the joke was on Dad.

That night, I dreamed about Crossfield burning, Mercy Warrener running for her life. I heard some notes of "Yankee Doodle" and saw a couple of rattlesnakes crawling together across a sunny rock. I dreamed a heck of a lot more than I could remember when I woke up in the middle of the night with my heart pounding. But I had the feeling that, at the end of the dream, Mercy had said something to me. I couldn't remember the exact words. But they had been something like "I do long for it so."

Long for what, Mercy? In the dark, at three in the morning, it seemed like an important question.

10

I was seeing Ileana that night. We had a date to go to the library.

This was not quite as bad as it sounds. The library had a small art gallery attached to it. It was open at night when there was an exhibition, which there was just then. And while I could have given it a pass, Ileana wanted to see it.

That was okay with me. Ileana could look at the art and I could look at her. Win-win, right? But Mom couldn't think of a nicer thing than for me to ask Turk to come along.

I wanted her with us like I wanted a pet scorpion following me around, but I knew Ileana would agree that I should at least ask. "She is your cousin, blah, blah, blah." And I was going to do the right thing.

So I went up to her attic and I said, "There's an art exhibit at the library tonight. Pretty lame. You probably don't want to go, right?"

And Turk said, "Sure. I'll check it out. What time?"

I told Ileana Turk was coming. She sighed and said, "Oh, good." Pause. "We are doing the right thing, my darling."

"You might just as well ask Justin, too," I said. "Darling."

It felt weird and good at the same time to say it.

"Justin has a Mercians meeting," Ileana said. "They always meet Fridays."

"You know, I was reading about those guys," I said. "They used to be the jenti militia. What do they do now?"

"You had better ask Justin about that," Ileana said. "They keep very much to themselves. The rest of us know little about them."

"Well, he can tell me about the old days, anyway," I said. "Maybe I'll impress him with how much I already know."

"Perhaps," Ileana said.

About seven-thirty, Ileana, Turk, and I got out of Ileana's limo in front of the library.

The New Sodom Public Library was over a hundred years old. It had granite walls and marble steps that were slippery as grease when it rained or snowed. Which may have been why, instead of a couple of stone lions guarding the front entrance, there were two huge, coiled rattlesnakes.

The snakes had their heads turned toward each other. Their mouths were open and their fangs were about a foot long. Under one were the words DON'T TREAD, and under the other it said ON ME. Officially, they were a tribute to New Sodom's Revolutionary War heroes, but a lot of people thought it was a warning about the steps.

The art gallery was a small wing off the main building.

Inside, the walls were white and the floors were dark polished wood.

Gadje and jenti were walking up and down, stopping in front of the paintings, which were mainly squares and oblongs of canvas that had been dipped in industrial sludge, I guess. They had titles like *The Third Time I Become the Sea,* and *Mourning of the Aesir*. Apart from Ileana, Turk, and me, everyone in the gallery was formally dressed, and at least forty years old.

Ileana set the pace for us. She cruised down one side of the exhibition and up the other. Then she stood in the center of the room and slowly turned around. I could tell she was really interested in all that canvas.

I was really interested in Ileana. But hand-holding was all we were going to be doing tonight. Still, her strong little hand gripped mine like our skins were fused.

Turk didn't seem to see the paintings at all. She was looking at everything else, checking out the height of the ceiling, measuring the walls with her eyes.

"Who do you have to know to get an exhibit here?" she said finally.

"Oh, there is a committee," Ileana said. "My mother is on it."

"Great," Turk said. "What are my chances of getting a show?"

"I am afraid you would have to be famous, Turk," Ileana said. "And it would be very helpful if you were dead. That is the sort of artist the committee prefers."

"Dead? I'll work on it," Turk said. But then she said, "Damn it. Isn't there anyplace in this town to get my stuff up?"

"There are a few private galleries," Ileana said. "But this

is the only public art space in New Sodom. It is too bad. It is such a small place for a town as large as New Sodom has become."

I remembered again what Mercy Warrener had longed for. She'd wanted a place where the two peoples of New Sodom could get together. And then it hit me. One of those old mills could be that place. It would be more than an art gallery. There could be space there for everything people wanted to do. Whatever Mercy Warrener would have wanted. Whatever Ileana might like. I smiled.

"You know, Turk was talking about those old factories across the river," I said. "Some towns have turned those kinds of places into art galleries."

"Yes. I am aware of that," Ileana said.

"I was thinking that a big building like that might be good for all sorts of things. You know, plays and stuff. Poetry readings, maybe."

Ileana didn't say anything for a minute. Her beautiful face was like the sky on a day when the clouds are flying by, and the sun comes and goes behind them, and the light and shadows are changing every second.

Finally, she said, "That would be very, very difficult here."

"Sure would be great, though," I said. "It could be a place for the jenti to sort of—you know—show what they can do."

"Not just jenti, Cuz," Turk said. "I have to get my stuff up, too."

"Kind of like Illyria for real," I said.

I figured this would be my best point. Last year, Ileana and Justin and I had spent time in Justin's basement building a private world we shared. We called it Illyria. We all had our own kingdoms. Ileana's had been all about the arts. Her two favorite characters were a couple of guys named Vasco and Anaxander, who were poets. If Ileana thought there was a chance to have something like that in the real world, she'd probably be on my side.

But Ileana shook her head.

"The jenti would never accept such a thing. Especially not in that place," she said.

"Why not?" Turk said. "It's perfect."

"And there's this," I said. "If you back it, a lot of people will come. I mean, let's face it. You're the princess around here."

"Let us go somewhere else," Ileana said. "I have something to tell you."

The chauffeur looked surprised when Ileana told him to take us to Crossfield.

"You must see something," Ileana told me and Turk. "It will help you to understand."

So we headed away from downtown and across the river. The limo bumped and thudded over the worn pavement of the bridge, and there were a couple of glints of light on the river below. But everything was dark in Crossfield.

"Stop here," Ileana told the chauffeur, and opened the door.

The chauffeur got out with us. He kept a few steps back, but there was no way he was going to let Ileana wander around by herself in Crossfield at night.

She led us to an open area between two of the old mills.

"One of these buildings would be right for your plan, I think," Ileana said.

"Yeah," Turk said. "I had that one on the left picked out."

"Now look down," Ileana said. "See where your feet are standing."

Her voice was funny. I didn't know if she was going to scream or cry.

We were standing on a bit of one of the narrow cobbled roads.

"Count the crossroads you can see from here," Ileana said.

"Twenty-three," I told her when I had done it.

"Twenty-five," Turk said.

"There is a jenti under every one of them. In some cases, more than one," Ileana said.

Turk and I looked at each other.

"The factories were built on top of these little roads," Ileana said. "It is as if the gadje of New Sodom tried to wipe us out twice."

"Did they know?" I said.

"Of course they knew," Ileana said. "In New Sodom nothing is ever forgotten."

"It was a long time ago," Turk said quietly.

"Not for the jenti," Ileana said. "Remember, we live a long time, when we are allowed to do so. Those who lie here might have been grandparents to our oldest. If they had not been killed, and buried here at these little crossroads with stakes through their hearts."

The way she said it made me want to cry.

"So now you know, dear Cody, why your beautiful idea is impossible," Ileana said. "The town of New Sodom wants to let Crossfield return to the dust. For the gadje it is a place of shame. For the jenti it is one of grief."

Turk nodded. Then she did something I never would have thought she'd ever do. She went over to Ileana and put her arms around her.

Why hadn't I thought of that?

And Ileana put her head on Turk's shoulder and sobbed.

I went over and put my arm across Ileana's shoulders. But it wasn't the same as holding her would have been.

When Ileana stopped crying, she hugged Turk. Then she hugged me so hard I couldn't breathe for a second. Jenti strength. Ileana was so tiny it was easy to forget that she was made of steel.

We got back into the limo and headed to New Sodom. The lights gleamed on its civilized, careful, historical streets.

But Crossfield was history, too. Mercy Warrener was history. Maybe everybody in New Sodom wanted Crossfield to sink back into the rocky dirt, but something was going to grow out of that dirt, sooner or later. Something always did.

II

The right thing. You grow up thinking there's always a right thing and a wrong thing. Then you start to realize that sometimes there's no right thing. Or that something might be wrong or right, depending on how it works out. Or that there's more than one right thing, and you have to make a choice. Like this time.

How could I not just forget the whole idea, now that I knew why nobody talked about Crossfield, and what had happened there? Ileana wanted me to. Justin would agree. Nobody but Turk really wanted to go ahead with this thing. Which was a pretty good clue that it was a bad idea.

But what good would leaving Crossfield alone do? It would always be a painful memory, no matter what else happened there. Wouldn't it be better to try to make something good grow in that place? Something that could make Ileana smile?

I didn't know. But, since I didn't, I thought the thing to do was to push it a little further and see what happened.

On Monday afternoon, Turk and I went down to the courthouse. We were going to find out who owned that mill.

The Gomorrah County Courthouse was a red brick monstrosity from the nineteenth century that had been designed to look like a castle by somebody who had never seen a castle. It had turrets and gargoyles and tall, narrow windows covered with iron bars. There were even ramparts that looked like they'd be good for pouring boiling oil down onto the cars driving by.

And of course it had dungeons.

Not real dungeons. Just offices. Three levels of them, all underground and all as small and dark as if the people who worked there were serving life sentences. But jenti aren't too hot for natural light, so it made a kind of sense to build it that way.

The hall of records takes up most of the first floor basement, but you can't find the documents about Crossfield there. To find those, you have to go to the annex, which is down on the third basement floor, at the end of the hall, behind an old-fashioned oak door, which is locked. The door has a window of frosted glass and the word ANNEX painted on it, and the word HOURS under that. Under that, there's nothing.

I knocked. Nothing happened. I knocked again. More nothing.

"Move over, Cuz," Turk said then, and started dragging one long, black pinkie nail all over the door.

"Turk, what is it with that scratching thing?" I asked.

"Back in the seventeenth century, they got so refined at the French court that they decided knocking was rude," Turk said. "So they started scratching at the door. And the longer the nail on your little finger was, the politer you were. I just like it."

"Doesn't seem to work any better," I said.

Turk started to scratch on the glass. Figure eights, spirals, curlicues, louder and faster. When she got to the zigzags, the door opened.

There was a tiny white-haired man glaring at us from behind the door. He was wearing a suit so old he looked like a character in a play.

"What do you want?" he snarled.

"Fire," Turk said.

The little man turned even paler.

"Get outta my way," he squeaked, and pushed past us. He went scuttling up the stairs, and the sound of his footsteps faded into the stones.

"Turk, that was the lowest lie I've ever heard you tell," I said.

"What lie?" Turk said. "All I did was say the word *fire*. Is it my fault if he draws false conclusions?"

We went into the annex. Turk shut the door behind us and locked it.

"Now, where's the stuff on Crossfield?" she said.

It wasn't hard to find it. There was one wall of shelves with big leather-bound books on them, and the words CROSSFIELD TITLES at the top. The only other things in the room were a wooden desk with a chair, a gooseneck lamp, and a big map on the wall opposite the books.

"Perfect," I said when I saw it.

It was Crossfield, divided up into lots and numbered. There were spidery words on some of them. SIMMONS MILL, PRESCOTT MILL, TURNER MILL.

Turk put one of her long nails on the Simmons Mill.

"That's the one we want," she said.

I made a note of the plat references and found the volume that matched up with it.

The deeds for that piece of land started in the 1650s. They ran through the seventeenth, eighteenth, nineteenth, and twentieth centuries, up till when the Simmons Mill had closed in the 1930s. Then they stopped.

The last owner listed was Grover Simmons.

"Eighty years nobody's paid any attention to that place," Turk said. "Grover Simmons has got to be long gone."

"Unless he's a jenti," I said. "Then he could show up tomorrow."

"No contact information, is there?" Turk said. "Running down ol' Grove ain't gonna be easy."

The office door rattled.

"Hey, let me in to my place," an old voice squeaked.

"See if you can find anything with old telephone numbers or addresses," Turk said. "I'll handle this."

I went searching through the shelves of books. Turk went over and leaned against the door.

"It's locked," Turk said.

"I know it's locked. Unlock it and let me in," the voice said.

"How do I know you're supposed to be in here?" Turk said.

"It's my office. You saw me in it. Let me in, you brats," the voice said.

"I can't see you now," Turk said. "How do I know you're the same guy?"

"Unlock the damn door and you'll see I'm the same guy," the voice said.

"Okay, I'll try," Turk said.

She rattled the lock for a long time.

"It's not working," she said.

"Turn the key!" the voice said.

"There's nothing here," I said.

Turk nodded.

"Oh, wait," she said. "I see a key. Hold on."

And she opened the door.

The little man pushed into the room. His eyes were glaring.

"You lied to me," he said. "You said there was a fire."

"No, I didn't," Turk said.

"Yes, you damn well did," the little man said.

"No. I said the word *fire* completely without context," Turk said. "You drew your own conclusions. It's part of a living art project I'm working on, throwing out a word and seeing how people react. You're the best one so far, by the way. Thanks for your help."

"Get out of my office and don't come back," the little man snarled.

"But wait," I said. "You've helped her with her homework. Now you have to help me with mine. My local history project. That's why I came here. Everybody says you know more about Crossfield than anybody else."

"Who said so?" the little man said. He sounded curious now.

"Well, everybody I asked about it," I said.

The little man crossed his arms.

"Well, maybe I do know more about Crossfield than anybody else," he said. "But that don't mean I have to tell what I know. Just because these are public records don't mean I have to shoot my mouth off. But anyway, what'd you wanna know?"

"I'm doing research on the Simmons Mill," I said. "And I don't find any records for the—the chain of title—after 1932. Why is that?"

"Chain of title? You're not here about the other thing?" the little man asked.

"What other thing?" Turk said.

"Nothin'. Forget about it," the little man said. "Anyway. The Simmons Mill. Maybe I can help you."

He pulled out the same volume that Turk and I had looked at and went slowly through the Simmons documents page by page.

Finally, he said, "It ain't here."

"So I was right," I said.

"Looks like it," the little man said.

"But somebody's got to own it, right?" I said.

The little man shrugged.

"Look, just end your research thing where the paper trail ends," he said. "1932. You lucked out, kid. Almost a hundred years you don't have to write about."

"Hey," I said. "I go to Vlad Dracul. If I turn in a paper that stops in 1932, I'll be lucky to get a C. Isn't there anything to update this with?"

"No, there ain't," he said. "That place could be in Frontier-land by now. Probly is."

"What's Frontierland?" I said.

"Aw, it's this old thing," the little man said. "See, Crossfield ain't really a part of New Sodom. I mean, it is, but it ain't. So there's this old law. Goes back to 1676 or something. When a piece of land in Crossfield stands empty too long, and nobody knows who owns it, anybody who wants it can homestead it. There's certain things you got to do to claim it, and you got to stay there a certain time, but then it's yours."

"Wow, that would make a great footnote," I said. "Can I see the document?"

The little man sighed, went to the bookshelves, and climbed up on a footstool.

"I shouldn't have to do this after what you kids done to me," he said. "I'm only doing it 'cause I'm a public servant."

"We appreciate it," Turk said. "And anyway, you were great."

"You really call that art?" the little man said. "Scaring someone?"

"Sure do," Turk said.

"Nutcase kid," the little man grunted. "Anyway, here it is."

AN ACT FOR THE TENURE OF EMPTY WASTES
When it shall hap that a farm or steading of any
sort shall be left untenanted for the time of three
yeares, and no owner be writ down in the towne
records, whoso shall tenant it and build thereon a
cabin or a wigwam, and plante corne, and dwell
for seven yeares upon it, shall have possession of
said farm or steading so long as it shall please him.
To keep or to sell, to leave unto descendants, and

to do all things that may be done with a farm or steading.

"They had all these places standing empty, see?" the little man said. "From the war. And nobody wanted to go back to Crossfield. So they tried to give it away, and that worked pretty good. Like you saw, there was somebody owned where Simmons Mill is up until the Great Depression."

"And this is still on the books?" Turk said.

"Yep," the little man said. "Just me and the rest of the guys in records know about it. Well, us and a few old-timers. Kind of a joke. Tear down the old mill and put up a wigwam. Plant some corn and stay there seven years and it's all yours."

"Gee, imagine somebody trying to do that now," Turk said.

The little man laughed.

"Good luck trying to grow corn in September," he said. "Anyway, that dirt's solid rock."

"Thanks," I said. "We'll do our best."

12

Turk and I drove out to our homestead in the empty wastes of Crossfield.

The mill looked different now that we almost sort of owned it. Those three floors of red brick looked exciting, like anything might happen there. And I was noticing details. The tall windows—those that were still there—had twenty-four panes of glass in them and were higher than a man, even a jenti. The main entrance had an arch with a flagpole hanging over it. And wrapped around the pole, all along its length, were two big brass rattlesnakes.

Turk noticed them, too.

"My kind of place," she said.

"Where are we going to put our cabin?" I asked.

"Wigwam," Turk said. "We're making a wigwam. It'll be my first art installation."

"So, our work but your art?" I said.

"Exactly," Turk smiled. "You can be my assistant. All the great artists have them."

I think it was the first time I'd ever seen her smile.

I was not smiling.

"Guess what, Turk?" I said. "You still don't have an assistant. You have a partner."

"Come on, Cuz," Turk said. "Get real. You can't do this. You don't even know what an arts center is supposed to look like. Without me, this is never going to happen."

"How many arts centers have you founded?" I asked.

"Almost one." Turk grinned. "But this stuff is my life. I know things. You don't."

I almost walked off. Turk's ego had found something bigger than Turk, just like Ileana had said, and it was my idea. Swell.

"Well, come on. Let's check out the inside," Turk said.

"I'm thinking," I said, turning away from her and back toward the river.

If I walked away, would that be the right thing? Wrong thing, I decided. In fact, I'd be damned if I'd quit. I'd had about all of Turk's ego I could take. This was my idea, and she couldn't have it. I'd hang in, fight her when I had to, and make this thing happen. I'd do it for Mercy, and for everybody in New Sodom like her.

The Act for the Tenure of Empty Wastes seemed like a clue that I was on the right track. I'd just have to deal with Turk, and make sure things went the way I wanted them to while she got her studio. I wouldn't get tied up in a tree house this time.

"Okay, *partner*. Let's take a look," I said.

We went in.

The floor was dark and dirty, and had holes where the big machines had been taken out. There were long lines of pillars running from wall to wall. And the smell of damp old dust was everywhere.

"Home sweet home," Turk said.

"It's going to take us a year just to get the floors swept," I said.

"Then it'll take a year," Turk said. "Only I'll bet it won't. I'll bet once we get the lights on and the windows replaced, people will be showing up to help. This is just waiting to happen. You can feel it."

I didn't feel anything except the dank cold, and maybe a kind of loneliness seeping out of the walls. Like the building missed the old days and wanted to be filled with people again. Or maybe I was just getting hungry.

Turk kept a flashlight in her car. Using it, we wandered through all the floors and found the bathrooms, some of which had very artistic vines growing in them. We found the old cafeteria, which had a good-sized kitchen attached to it. There was an old walk-in freezer and a couple of old-fashioned iron ranges. We went into the dispensary, which still had its red cross on the door, though nothing was left on the other side of it. Down in the basement, we found the old furnace, the generator, and a pair of big old turbines.

"I knew this place would have its own electricity," Turk said. "Turbines. When we get those working again, we can do anything."

More and more, I was getting the feeling that the Simmons Mill had been a world all its own. And that it could be again.

I wanted to do everything at once. Sweep, fix the windows, get the lights back on and the furnace working, then go to Ileana and say, "It's yours."

I must have been imagining it really hard, because just then a voice started singing in jenti. It was a powerful, dark voice, and it came from somewhere above us.

"Damn," Turk said. "What is that noise?"

"Jenti music," I said.

"Come on," Turk said. "Let's find out who's in our place."

We climbed up the metal stairs that led to the second floor, then to the third. The sounds of the music got louder and louder. I was almost sure I knew who was making them. But what would he be doing here?

At one end of the third floor was a big wooden door. It probably led to offices. On it, handwritten on a long sheet of paper, was this:

> *I fly.*
> *High above this small, smug place which I hate. Where the streetlights shine down on the bland roofs of Cape Cod cottages and ranch houses, I fly at night.*
> *I fly.*
> *I fly under the sun, daring it to roast me, casting my shadow on the streets. I swoop low over the trees, over the small yards that contain the small lives.*
> *They pretend not to see me, the gadje. But I span twenty meters. My shadow falls on them and they tremble.*

Sometimes I shriek my war cry.

We are not supposed to do any of this here in New Sodom. There are civic codes against flying without a license. They look like they were written for airplanes. But they were written for us.

We are supposed to behave ourselves here, we of the jenti. It is an old tradition that we do not upset the gadje.

I no longer care.

Gadje, jenti, they are all alike to me.

And I cannot love this place. I will not love it.

I fly because it is the one thing left to me.

When I can find one, I fly into a thunderhead. The winds in the tall tower of cloud tear at me, send me climbing high on a blast of air fast as the coming of a new hate. I struggle just to keep flying. To keep from being torn apart. The air rushes me up, up, until ice forms on my wings. Until the air becomes too thin to breathe, and a black shroud drops over my mind.

Then I plummet. Thrown by the wind, blinded by the clouds and my own oxygen-starved brain, I fall through the maelstrom, through the lightning. The thunder shakes my bones.

Then at last I fall out of the storm. I may be any-where by then. The storm moves, and takes me where it wills. No, not where it wills. It wills nothing for me. It does not even know I am there.

In rain or hail, in wind and shadows, I try to figure out where I am. Then I fly in the direction I came from.

No matter how tired and beaten I am, I never stop until I return to New Sodom. That is my game. I will not allow myself to rest.

If the day comes when I fall exhausted from the sky and lie on some patch of stranger ground, gasping out my last breath, slowly changing back into my human form, let it be. If I never find that last flight, let that be. I do not seek the storm because I want to die.

I seek the storm because it is my only home.

"Oooh. A tortured soul," Turk said.

I tried the door. It swung open without a sound.

The singing stopped.

There were a couple of old couches, a ratty carpet, a few chairs, a low table, and a few other things. On one wall was a huge poster that showed an old castle and said LANGUEDOC. Another showed a deep river valley and said RHEINFELLS.

"None of this is left over from the 1930s," I said. "It's too new."

"Some homeless guy's place, I'll bet," Turk said.

"That's a very good description," a voice behind us said.

We turned and saw Gregor glaring at us. He had come in from the next room. Behind him, I could see a music stand.

He looked embarrassed. Anyway, his pale skin was dark. On the other hand, his fangs were out. Maybe he was just blushing.

"What are you doing here?" he said.

"Taking over," said Turk.

"This is my place," Gregor said. "You are taking nothing over here."

"Wrong," Turk said. "We're the new homesteaders."

"Whatever that means, it means nothing," Gregor said. "These rooms are mine."

"The hell they are," Turk said. "We own this."

"You lie," Gregor said. "No one owns this."

"They do now," Turk said.

Gregor and Turk were glaring at each other like they were ready to start punching.

"Hold on," I said. "Look, Gregor. Turk and I did some research on this place. It turns out that nobody owns it. And according to an old New Sodom law, anybody who does certain things can claim it. That's what Turk's talking about."

"There are others of these old buildings," Gregor said. "Take one of them and leave me in peace."

"Sorry, Gregor, it's ours," I said.

"Just a couple of old Yankee homesteaders," Turk added.

The way Turk and Gregor were looking at each other was scary. *Hatred* was too weak a word for it.

Gregor walked over to a window and forced it open. The wood screeched in the frame, and a breath of fresh air blew into the room. "Out there is everything," he said. "I give it to you. Why do you want this pile of dirty bricks anyway? What good is it to anyone but me?"

"I'm going to turn it into an arts center," Turk said. "And a studio for me. Deal with it."

"That is such a stupid idea in so many ways that I cannot begin to scorn it," Gregor said.

"Try," Turk said. "I'm fascinated by stupid arguments."

"In the first place, this building would need millions of dollars to renovate," Gregor said. "Do you have millions of dollars? In the second, it is not intended for such a purpose and will never work well. In the third, no one in New Sodom wants such a thing. Hardly anyone. No one but you, really. So who would fill this art center, and with what? Those are the first of my stupid arguments. Now let me hear your brilliant explanation of why I am wrong."

"The money's a problem," Turk said. "But the big cost is the purchase price. And there isn't one. All we have to do is get to work. And we don't have to do it all at once. Once we get lights and heat on in here, and get the place cleaned out, we'll be ready for some shows. And when people see what we've got, and what's going on, they'll go home thinking about what they can do here."

"Yes. I can understand why you would entertain this fantasy," Gregor said. "You think you are an artist and intellectual. But you, Cody Elliot, I do not understand. You are no more interested in the arts than a duck is in baseball. So why are you doing this?"

I didn't see any reason to mention Mercy Warrener. Even to Gregor, doing something for a woman who died in 1820 would probably seem a little weird. So I said, "Ileana."

"Ah. Of course," Gregor said. "What does she think of your idea?"

"She says it'll never work," I said. "She says the jenti won't want anything to do with it. Because of what happened here."

"And still you go ahead," Gregor said. "Why?"

"Because I think she'll love it when it's real," I said.

"You think it would be Illyria for her," Gregor said.

"You know about Illyria?" I said.

"I have known Ileana Antonescu much longer than you, gadje," Gregor said. "She has told me about Illyria."

He shook his head. "Gadje, you are in so much deeper than you know. If the princess does not want you to do this, it is not only because of what is buried here in Crossfield. I think she is also trying to protect you."

"From what?" Turk said.

"This is an old town by American standards," Gregor said. "It has secrets within its secrets. And you are a fool if you think those who keep them wish them to be revealed."

"Ooh, I'm getting chills," Turk said. "But you're going to have to come up with a better story than that to scare me off."

But I knew Gregor could be telling the truth. This place was all about old secrets and hidden connections. Sometimes, I thought New Sodom should have been built underground.

"If that is what you think, I will enjoy watching you find out how wrong you are," Gregor said. "It will be amusing to watch you fail."

He opened the door and tore down the poem that had hung there. He rolled it up and stuffed it in his jacket.

"I want only my posters and my music," he said. "The rest of these things you can deal with. Brilliantly, I am sure."

"Gregor, you don't have to leave," I said all of a sudden.

"Yes, he does," Turk said.

"No, he doesn't," I said. "This is supposed to be an arts center for everybody. Well, he's somebody and he's doing art. There's room for him."

Gregor looked at me like I'd sprouted a pair of leathery wings.

"Why?" He said it like I'd said something really stupid.

"Because it's the right thing to do," I said.

"No," Turk said.

"Yes," I said. "He was here first. Deal with it."

"He doesn't even want to stay," Turk said.

But Gregor ignored her.

"If I help you, I must keep this room," he said.

"That's the point," I said.

"Two minutes ago, you said my idea was stupid," Turk said.

"It is stupid," Gregor agreed. "But I know Cody Elliot. His stupid ideas have been known to work. I must reluctantly deal with that possibility. And what do I stand to lose? If, even with my help, you fail, I keep my place here. If, because of my help, you succeed, I still keep it."

"And all of a sudden the Crossfield thing doesn't bother you?" Turk said.

"Of course it bothers me," Gregor said. "He bothers me. You bother me worst of all. But losing this place bothers me more. So you have your first supporter."

Turk looked furious with Gregor and with me. Finally, she said, "Just as long as you remember who's in charge."

"As if you would let anyone forget," Gregor said.

"Damn right," Turk said.

"It's not about who's in charge," I said.

Gregor didn't answer. Or maybe he did.

He went and stood backward on the sill of the open window, and threw out his arms. Behind them, his big, dark wings spread out and blocked out the sun. The rest of his body tightened up, ready for flying. His chest stretched against his shirt and his dark eyes glittered. He spread his lips and showed his fangs.

"Shall we begin Saturday?" he said in the same deep voice he sang in.

Turk didn't answer. She crossed her arms and tried to look cool, but she was staring at those big, powerful wings on the other side of the glass. I think she was fascinated.

"Nine o'clock," I said.

"Do not be late, gadje," Gregor replied, and threw himself off the sill.

He hung there, framed by the window, then flapped once and was carried up out of sight.

Turk couldn't help it. She went to the window and stared up, following Gregor's path.

There was a tall cloud that looked like it might flatten out into a thunderhead off to the north. I saw a flash of Gregor as he headed toward it.

"Damn," Turk said. "I wish I could do that."

13

We told Mom and Dad we had found some space for Turk in Crossfield, but it would need some repairs.

They were surprisingly cool about the whole thing. Mom was so glad that Turk and I were doing something together that she didn't care what it was. Dad was relieved Turk wasn't nagging him to buy her a mill. He had no curiosity at all about what we were doing.

I figured there was no need to lay the whole thing on them until we'd gotten a lot of work done and showed them we were serious. There would be time later to let them know they had a couple of pioneers living with them. So we were on our own, at least for now.

Justin and Ileana were a different story.

"That sounds crazy," Justin said when I told him.

"But homesteading," I said. "Living history. Resurrecting the past. A-plus from Gibbon."

Justin gave me a stony look.

"What about your Mercians?" I said. "All those old-time families. Would any of them be interested in helping out?"

"Nope," Justin said.

"Civic improvement," I said. "Community—things. Isn't that what you do?"

"No," Justin said. "Anyway, not that kind."

"Well, what do you do, just sit around and wait for the redcoats to attack?" I said.

"Look, Cody. Just don't do it. Please," Justin said.

And when I told Ileana, she looked at me over clasped hands and said, "I hope that you will fail."

Turk went crazy buying things that week. Buckets, mops, paper towels—if it cleaned, she loaded up on it. Our garage started to look like a janitorial supply store.

"Where are you getting all the money for this?" I asked when she came home Thursday with the 179th load of sponges.

"Art, Cuz," she said. "My brilliant career pays for it all. I sold two big pieces just before I came. But they're nothing compared to what I'm going to do when my art center's up and running."

"Ah, yes. *Your* art center," I said. "The living flame to your eternal genius."

"Yeah. Something like that," Turk said.

I wasn't around much while Turk was busy with all this. I spent most of my afternoons with Justin, getting help with my math, or upstairs in my room trying to figure out on my own whether the giant panda was taxonomically a bear or a raccoon (no fair checking the DNA) and why, in either case, a meat-eater had evolved into a bamboo-eater without giving up carnivorous dentition. Fun times.

Or I was in the special collections room with Mercy, going over her journal, page by page, feeling that strange connection that came from looking at her spidery hand-writing. Feeling her life touching mine.

To make sure that Ms. Shadwell didn't discover Mercy's journal and take it away to be cataloged or something, I always hauled out several of the ephemera collections along with it and pretended to look into them from time to time. This worked. When I told her the title of my report was *Comparative Ephemera of New Sodom in Colonial Times,* she was as happy as a clam at high tide.

So Mercy remained my secret.

The more I reread her words, the more questions I had. Some of them were things like "You actually ate robin pie?" and one was "Who was that lover you missed so much for the rest of your life?" But most of them were about the Mercians.

I was really interested in those guys. I made a note of every mention of them in Mercy's journal. She wrote about them fairly often during the Revolution, and then never again until the War of 1812. Then it was just:

August 8, 1812
    The New Sodom Militia, Mercians and gadje alike, have voted not to go to the new war. The whole town do be against this fight with England.

After that, nada, zip, zilch.

Mercians. Whatever they had been, they were still

around. But if they weren't a militia, what were they, and why wouldn't Justin talk about them? There couldn't be anything wrong with them, or Justin wouldn't be one. But why act like a conspiracy when you're not?

Then Saturday came and I had other things to think about.

When we drove up to the mill at nine, Gregor was already waiting. The back of the Volkswagen was filled with cleaning stuff, gardening tools, and a couple of hatchets.

I had something of my own, tucked into a Styrofoam cooler, for later. A surprise for Turk and Gregor.

"The first thing is to stake our claim," Turk said. "Then clean up."

Gregor sneered. "You had better use a different word than *stake* if you want my help," he said.

I handed him a hatchet. "Come on, Gregor. You and me. Let's get the poles for the wigwam."

But Turk picked up the other hatchet.

"I'm doing the wigwam," she said. "You start the corn patch."

"But I read up on the wigwam," I said. "I pulled some stuff off the net."

"So did I," Turk said. "And I'm smarter than you. Dig."

"She is right, you know," Gregor said. "She is smarter."

"Wigwam," I said. "We'll all help."

We walked down to the river, where some thickets of small trash trees were growing. We found some young ones that were about the right size, and flexible enough to bend.

"We need sixteen for the basic frame," Turk announced. "And a lot more besides that for crosspieces."

Gregor didn't say anything. He just took his hatchet, slashed at a tree, and cut it down with two strokes.

"Fifteen," he said.

"It's too big," Turk said. "You can't bend them if they're that thick."

"You cannot bend them. I can," Gregor said, and cut down the next.

"Stop it," Turk said. "Cut the small ones."

"I will cut the ones I think are best," Gregor said.

And that was all it took. Turk and Gregor got into a long fight about poles, who was in charge, and why the other one was stupid. End of tree-chopping.

"Excuse me," I said. "Some of us showed up to work." And I took Turk's hatchet and went off where I couldn't hear them so well.

I loved cutting the trees down, seeing my stack of saplings get bigger, and if it took me more than two whacks to get one, so what? The sun was bright, the air was warm, the breeze was coming up off the river, and I was having fun.

When I had a dozen, I checked back with Turk and Gregor. They had added one more to the two Gregor had cut when I left.

"Don't cut that one, it's too thick," Turk was shouting.

"The only thing that is too thick is your head," Gregor said.

I wondered cheerfully which of them would use the hatchet on the other first.

"Hey, guys," I said. "If I end up building this thing myself, I get to make the rules about who gets in."

"Take this cousin of yours and help her to start the corn patch," Gregor growled. "I will finish here in an hour and I will join you."

"Like hell," Turk said.

"Come on, Turk," I said. "He's right. Neither of you is getting anything done."

"One hour," Turk said. "And the poles had better be the right size."

Turk and I carried my poles up to the mill.

She was still grumbling—that's a polite word for it—about having to help with the corn patch.

"Anyway, doing that will take all day," she snarled. "I want to get the wigwam up, not scratch around in the dirt for some corn that isn't going to come up anyway."

"You're not thinking," I said. "The act says, 'plant corn.' But it doesn't say what defines a corn patch. It doesn't even say that it has to grow corn. All it says is, we have to plant it. And I've got what we need."

"I got everything we need," Turk said. "I bought hoes and seeds and stuff."

"Did you buy the dead fish?" I said.

I opened my cooler.

"Voila," I said. "Twelve dead fish. That's how the Pilgrims fertilized their corn. One dead fish to each three kernels."

"Who told you?"

I wasn't going to tell Turk that Mercy Warrener had mentioned it in her journal.

"A friend," I said. "Dig."

Turk cheered up a little at the prospect of handling dead fish, and we got to work. By the time we had a dozen holes dug, filled with dead fish and corn, and mounded up, Gregor was coming up from the river dragging a load of poles stripped of their bark. So we had more than we needed.

We'd brought sandwiches and drinks from home. We

had lunch, and Turk and Gregor fought about how to do the wigwam. This was really very interesting, because Indians made wigwams for centuries before we showed up, and the technique is not exactly secret. When I was done eating, I got started.

To do a wigwam, the first thing is to make a circle on the ground. Take a stick, pound it in someplace, then tie a rope to it and trace your circle with your heel as you pull the rope around. Then dig little holes at regular intervals around the circle for the poles you're going to use. That's it.

And if you do it on the opposite side of a building from where the people who are supposed to be working with you are having their fight, you can get it all done before they show up.

"I am not ashamed to be better than you," Gregor was saying as they came around the corner of the mill.

"I didn't say you were ashamed to be better, I said you people are ashamed to be vampires," Turk said.

"Same thing," Gregor said. "Vampire equals better than gadje. And we are not ashamed of it."

"So why do I never see anybody flying around?" Turk said.

"I 'fly around,' as you put it," Gregor said, "whenever I wish."

"I mean other people," Turk said. "The rest of you. You'll show off your money, you'll show off your brains. But you won't show off the thing that makes you different."

"Possibly we have more important things to do than to amuse you," Gregor said.

Clearly, these two had not finished their fascinating discussion.

"Hey," I said. "I've started on the wigwam. Bring the poles."

Turk stopped fighting with Gregor and walked all around the work I'd done.

"Who told you we were going to put it here?" Turk said, looking at the holes I'd made.

"Dang. Forgot to ask your permission," I said. "Bring the poles."

"I was going to put it by the entrance," Turk said.

"I got tired of waiting for you to finish snarking at Gregor," I said.

"Well, I want it at the front," Turk said.

Gregor had been looking at the plans.

"Hah. Eight sticks in a circle. Nothing but a basket turned upside down," Gregor said, ignoring Turk. "Simple."

"It had better be simple if you're going to work on it," Turk said.

Gregor disappeared around the corner and came back with the poles.

"With my *vampire* strength, things will go quickly," he said.

"But——" Turk opened her mouth, then bit down on unsaid words.

"Score," I thought.

While Turk and I struggled to get one pole into the ground, Gregor forced the other seven into their holes. Jenti strength. But there was something more going on. Intensity. I figured he was trying to show Turk how much better he was.

When the poles were pointing to the sky like bony fingers, we tied them into pairs so they made arches. Gregor bent them together like they were straws, and Turk and I tied the knots. We had the frame of our wigwam, and it hadn't taken an hour.

Then we took the next eight poles and did the same thing. Now we had a pretty complicated framework. We made hoops.

The hoops were four rings that ran around the outside of the framework. We made them by tying the saplings we had left together in twos and threes. Then we lashed them to every pole they crossed. We finished just as the first cool breeze of evening came up from the river.

I was panting. So was Turk. Even Gregor was breathing hard. But the thing was real. It didn't look like a playhouse or a joke. People had lived in these things, and they had been strong enough and warm enough to protect a whole family against a Massachusetts winter.

I crawled inside and looked up through the lattice of poles we'd made. The sky was turning a deeper blue, and the sun was just above the trees.

It hit me for the first time: We'd done it. We'd actually homesteaded this place. We'd made it ours.

"It feels right," I said. "It feels like we belong here."

"Gadje," Gregor said. "Gadje fantasies. You think you are pioneers now. Cowboys."

"What's your fantasy?" I asked.

"My fantasy is that you two forget about this place and never come here again," Gregor said.

"You're right," Turk said. "That is a fantasy."

"Anyway, we're done here," I said. "Let's go home."

"You want a ride, Gregor?" Turk said.

Gregor laughed and threw out his arms, jumped into the

air higher than any gadje ever could, and changed. His wings unfolded, and he hovered over us. He seemed to fill the sky.

"Tell me when you want to work again," he shouted down.

Gregor beat the air three times and pushed himself up to the level of the mill roof. He tilted his wings to catch the river breeze, and rose a little more. Then, screaming something in high jenti, he angled away from us and flew toward the night.

"I guess that meant no," I said.

14

The next week was busy. With eight hundred tons of home-work to do every night, I didn't have a chance to get out to Crossfield. Neither did Turk. I noticed that, smart as she was, she had to spend almost as much time as I did cracking her skull open to put into it everything that Vlad said was sup-posed to be there.

So it wasn't until Saturday that Turk and I went out to find that somebody had burned down our wigwam frame. There was nothing left but a circle of soot, ash, and the stumps of blackened sticks.

The corn patch had been dug up, too.

Turk said some really choice things in Spanish when she saw the remains. I stuck to English and jenti.

"I wish I knew who did it," Turk said when she'd calmed down a little. "I'd murder them."

"Ah, hell, take your pick," I said. "Some gadje who doesn't want us doing this, some jenti who hates gadje, some jerk who thought it would be fun."

Gregor came around the corner of the mill. "So you have seen it," he said.

"Hard to miss," I said.

"It happened last night," he said. "I was out flying and I saw the smoke."

"Did you see who did it?" Turk asked.

"I am not certain," Gregor said. "I have my suspicions."

"Who do you think it was?" I asked.

"I will not speak without more proof," Gregor said. "And anyway, the important thing is to see that it does not happen a second time."

"Great idea," Turk said. "How?"

"Someone must be here every night from now on," Gregor said.

"Who's going to do that?" I said.

"We will take turns," Gregor said. "My friends and I."

"You have friends?" Turk said.

I knew Gregor's friends. They were all guys from Europe who lived in the dorms.

"The school's just going to let you guys stay out all night?" I said.

"We live in dorms, gadje, not prisons," Gregor said. "Yes, we can do this if we use a little care. And there will be four of us. That will be enough. More than enough."

"Hey, we can help," Turk said. "I can get out any time I want to."

"You will be of no value in this," Gregor said. "If what happened means what I think it does, more than a wigwam is in danger." He slapped the wall of the mill.

"Then I am definitely going to be here," Turk said.

"It is already decided," Gregor said. "You must trust me."

"That'll be the day," Turk said.

"Look, you stupid gadje, I told you there were things going on that you do not know about. What happened last night was—come and see what I have been doing about it."

He led us into the mill. Back in one corner, he had piled up stones and dirt about three feet deep. They had been carefully piled, and bordered with rock, like an indoor garden. In the middle was a stack of new poles.

There were three guys standing around, covered with dirt and holding the tools Turk had bought. I knew them slightly. On my first day at Vlad, they had helped Gregor try to take me apart, and had come close to doing it. Since then we hadn't had much to say to each other.

"Ilie Nitzu, Constantin Trifa, and Vladimir Bratianu," Gregor said to Turk. "From now on, they will help."

They nodded to Turk.

I wasn't sure I liked this. Keeping Turk from jerking my idea in one direction was trouble enough. Now it looked like Gregor wanted to drag it in another, and had brought his friends to help him do it.

"Hold on," I said. "We need to talk about this."

"More talk?" Gregor said.

"Yeah," I said. "You guys aren't exactly members of the Cody Elliot fan club, so why should I trust you? You say there's some kind of mysterious threat to this place, but you won't say what it is, so why should I believe you? And let's face it, you may have your own agenda that you haven't told me anything about, so why should I let you?"

"Good questions," Gregor said.

"Yeah," Turk said. "You're getting smarter, Cuz."

"Here is the only answer I can give you," Gregor said. "I swear on my honor as a duke of the jenti that I really believe there may be a serious threat to this place. I swear that I have no ulterior motive. And I swear that each of us will do what he can to make this stupid idea of yours come to be. If it does not, it will be your fault, not ours. Believe me, and we can go on together. Say you do not, and I will send my friends away. But decide."

Duke of the jenti? I'd known Gregor was pretty high up in the jenti world, but I'd never known he had a title. But that didn't matter. I might not like Gregor much, but if there was one thing I was sure of, it was that he'd never break his word to me. He'd be ashamed to fail in front of Cody Elliot.

"Let's get to work," I said.

"Wait a minute," Turk said.

"No, no more waiting minutes," Gregor said. "Either help, or give orders. If we like them, we will take them." He turned to his friends. "Come. We are going to be Indians now."

Ilie, Vladimir, and Constantin grinned like wolves and picked up the poles.

By the end of the morning, we had our new wigwam frame up. It looked sad and lonely in the corner of the factory, but it would be safe enough. That's what we told ourselves.

I went outside and looked at what was left of the corn

patch. I put a few of the mounds back together. Some had corn and some didn't. It didn't matter. It just had to look like we were back in the corn business.

While I worked, I went over what Gregor had told us, and not told us. I was pretty sure someone must be watching us. If they hadn't been before, they probably were now. And Gregor had an idea who it was, even if he wasn't saying.

It made me curious. I wondered if whoever it was had left some evidence.

I walked slowly around the mill looking for anything that might have been dropped. While I was doing that, the windows of the mill began to screech open. Frames that had been painted shut back in the 1930s were being forced open by the jenti. And when they had them open, things began to fly through them. Old machine parts, mummies of dead rats, and bolts of rotten cloth came sailing out in every direction.

Since I didn't want to get hit by a cast iron flywheel or a hundred-year-old rat, I went inside.

Turk was sitting inside the wigwam with her legs pulled up. She was shouting at the jenti, who were ignoring her while they cleared the floor junk.

"Go amuse your cousin," Gregor said when I came in. "I think she has not enough people to shout at."

"No, thanks," I said. "I'm on a secret mission."

It had crossed my mind that maybe whoever had burned the wigwam and torn up the corn had paid a visit to the inside of the building, too. I dodged past the jenti and went up to the second floor, then the third. Everything looked just the way it had. Dirty and cluttered.

I got the flashlight out of Turk's car and went down the basement steps.

The door at the bottom hung open.

Turk and I had been down here precisely once. And when we left, I had closed the door. I remembered that clearly, because it had been so hard to pull shut. Now the door handle was lying on the floor, snapped off.

We had had company. Maybe we still did.

"Hey!" I shouted. "Down here. Now."

Turk, Gregor, and his guys appeared at the top of the stairs.

"Aha," Gregor said. "Interesting."

He came down and joined me.

"Last night, when I saw the fire, I decided to stay here until morning," Gregor said. "About an hour later, I thought I heard the outer doors open and close. But when I looked, I saw no one."

"So someone's interested in this basement after what, eighty years?" I said. "Let's see if we can find out why."

We looked at everything: the storerooms, the generators, the old circuit board. But nothing looked different.

Nothing I could see.

But Ilie nudged Gregor and pointed with his chin.

"Ah," Gregor said, and added something in jenti.

Constantin, Ilie, and Vladimir all started whispering, and I didn't understand more than two words of it. Damn.

"What, what?" Turk demanded.

I shined the light where the jenti were staring with their see-in-the-dark eyes.

At first I didn't see anything. But when I moved the beam around, I could see some faint lines scratched into the brick above one of the storerooms.

No matter how I shifted the flashlight, the lines didn't

make any sense. But there were too many of them to be random. And they couldn't have been done in a few seconds. They were too elaborate. If they looked like anything, they looked like a large, loopy *Y* with some angular squiggles at the bottom.

So what were they and why were they here? And who had put them here, and when, and did it matter?

"Talk," Turk said to Gregor. "What do you see?"

"Nothing that concerns a gadje," Gregor said.

"If it's in this building it concerns me," I said. "Tell us what it is."

"It is an old bit of jenti graffiti," Gregor said. "Someone who worked here in the old days must have put it there."

"What does it mean?" I asked.

"Who can say now?" Gregor said. "Some private joke, perhaps."

"A laugh riot," Turk said. "But I don't believe you."

Neither did I. I could feel the Rustle going on around me.

That mark. We didn't expect to see it here.

No. But it is here.

Why?

It doesn't matter. We find out who did it.

Yes. And then we break their wings.

That was what I thought was going on, all at the same time, as Gregor and his boys shifted quietly from one foot to the other. But without being able to see them clearly, I couldn't be sure. The only thing that I was clear about was that they were angry.

"Well, we are done here," Gregor said suddenly. "Tomorrow we will finish the cleaning. But only if you tell us to do so, of course."

"I'm not leaving until you tell me what's really going on," Turk said.

But Gregor was already leading his guys up the stairs. Their feet clumped heavily up the steps, and I heard the big front doors swing open and closed.

"Come on," I said. "These batteries won't last forever."

Outside, the night was warm and the first stars were coming out. It would have been a perfect night to be with Ileana. But she was busy tonight. Busy as in "I'm mad at you." So instead I was getting ready to go home with my least favorite relative after a happy day spent cleaning out a derelict building and, for all I knew, messing around with some ancient jenti curse. How did I get so lucky?

Overhead, Gregor, Vladimir, Ilie, and Constantin were all flapping and gliding around the mill.

"Hey, you said you were going to guard this place," Turk shouted.

"We are," Gregor said. "From up here. Go home, gadje."

So Gregor thought someone was watching the mill, too. Someone he wanted to see him and his friends.

Turk shouted something else to him, but he lifted himself up beyond the sound of her voice, and the others followed.

"Some guys have all the luck," I said.

"What?" Turk said.

"Nothing," I said. "Come on. We've got a fascinating evening of homework ahead."

We got into the Volkswagen and drove off.

As we were crossing the river, Turk said, "That was a weird day."

"Like many in New Sodom," I said.

"Those guys who hang with him, they're like servants more than friends. They hardly ever talked."

"They just didn't want to talk to us," I said.

"Bunch of snobs," Turk said.

"Takes one to know one," I said.

"How does he get them to do what he wants?" Turk said.

"He's from an important family," I said. "That's all I know."

"Oh, yes. Duke Gregor. What a joke," Turk said. "What's that supposed to mean, anyway?"

"I don't know," I said.

"Hey," Turk said. "Do you think he put those marks there to try and scare us?"

"Are you scared?" I asked her.

"Nooo," Turk said slowly, like I'd asked her a very dumb question.

"There's your answer," I said. "If Gregor wanted to scare you, he would."

"Hah," Turk said.

"All I know is, I'm pretty sure Gregor's not telling the truth," I said. "I think those marks meant something important when they were made. The question is whether they're new or not."

Turk shook her head.

"I don't like it, Cuz. I don't like any of it."

15

But whatever Turk didn't like, she had no cause for complaint on Sunday. She complained anyway, of course. But the jenti tore through the second and third floors of the mill all morning while Turk told them they were doing it all wrong, and Gregor told her to kindly shut up.

An avalanche of junk came through the windows and bounced and crashed onto the ground around the mill. By noon, the outside looked like a yard sale at an insane asylum, but inside the floors were clear and you had a sense of just how big this building really was.

"Not so ugly now," Gregor said.

"It feels like something could happen here, all right," I said.

"It will," Turk said, passing out brooms. "It had better. Sweep, creeps."

We knocked down cobwebs, swept the floor three times, and dusted the walls. The funny thing was, it started to feel like fun. We broke up into two teams without anyone saying, "Hey, let's break up into two teams!" Turk, Gregor, and Constantin were one. The other was Ilie, Vladimir, and me. We each took half the long room and tried to beat the other getting done first.

When we were finished with that, we took a break for drinks.

"These walls are good brick," Vladimir said, wiping his mouth. "Washed and scrubbed, they would be handsome."

"We don't have a ladder that long," Turk said. "I'll have to get one."

Vladimir jumped to the top of a wall and hung there by one hand, clutching the bricks.

"You have brush and water, please?" he said.

"Brushes, sure, but no water yet," Turk said. "We can't go running down to the river for a bucket every few minutes."

"There is water," Gregor said. "Or was once. See, there are sinks along that wall."

There were six sinks about the size of wading pools. Gregor walked over to one and tried to turn the taps. Constantin, Vladimir, Ilie, Turk, and I all joined him at the other sinks. They were like iron. Actually, I suppose, they were iron. Anyway, they didn't want to move. We all stood there grunting and twisting, and finally one of Ilie's let go. Then one of Gregor's. In a few more minutes, every one of the jenti's faucets was twirling back and forth like it was 1930 again. Turk's and mine were still frozen solid.

"You permit me to try?" Constantin said to me.

Gregor just walked over to Turk and stood beside her.

"Take your best shot," she said, giving up.

Gregor and Constantin growled deep in their throats and leaned on the taps, and in a minute they had rejoined the Land of the Working.

Then we all went outside to the shutoff valve.

The shutoff valve was big enough that two of us could get on it at once. Gregor and Vladimir tried to turn it, and it was interesting to watch. I'd never seen jenti faces get so red before. They made space for Constantin and Ilie. That valve didn't even budge.

Finally, when they were looking exhausted, I said, "I know I only have the body of a weak and feeble gadje, but let me in there," and they did.

If this was supposed to be the part where my one little extra bit of strength made the difference, somebody forgot to tell somebody about it. Pretty soon, I was as wiped out as they were.

We all lay on dry grass and panted.

Turk walked over and looked at it.

"Oh, man," she said. "Wouldn't you know it?"

"What's the matter?" I said. "Apart from the fact that nothing's working."

Turk didn't answer. She just leaned all her weight on the valve and made grunting sounds. Then the valve gave a short skreak and began to move.

"Somebody stuck a British fitting on the pipe," she said. "It turns the other way."

"You are joking," Gregor said. "Anyway, how do you recognize such a thing?"

"I do art," Turk said. "I did a whole network of pipes

and faucets once and entered it in a show in Seattle. Called it *Water You Doing*. Great title. Didn't win, though."

"You have been—intelligent," Gregor said, dragging the words out of himself.

"Duh." Turk shrugged.

From inside the mill came a sound like dragons roaring, trying to get out.

"What is such noise?" Vladimir said.

I swear he jumped.

"Air in the pipes," I said.

"Let's go see our water," Turk said.

Inside, the faucets were trembling and spitting, coming back to life one at a time. Water came spewing out in brown, angry jolts, along with grumbling air that hadn't moved in seventy years or more.

"You know, some of these drains could be clogged," I said.

"Thought of it, Cuz," Turk said. She produced a plunger and stood there holding it like a scepter.

Sure enough, the sink right in front of us began to back up.

"Permit me?" Constantin said, and held out his hand.

"Sure," Turk said, handing him the plunger.

Constantin worked the plunger up and down and side to side, and gave a heave that sent water flying all over us.

The drain gulped greedily, and the water went down in the most beautiful swirl I'd ever seen.

In an hour, the air was gone from the pipes and the water was running clean. Relatively clean. Almost clean. Clean enough for what we had to do next, which was wash the walls.

You have no idea how fast four jenti can wash the walls of a hundred-and-fifty-year-old New England mill unless you've seen them do it. Room by room and floor by floor they scrubbed. None of them spoke except to call for another bucket. Turk and I ran buckets of fresh water to them while they hung on the walls, one or two to each, and made long, sweeping strokes that changed the color of the bricks to dark, warm red.

Vladimir licked one of the bricks and said, "Not bad. If it were made of blood, I would like it."

By now it was getting dark inside the mill. We closed everything up. By the time we were done, the sun was throwing patterns of squares all the way across the bottom floor. They made our half-done wigwam glow.

"I never thought it was going to be this easy," Turk said.

"Not so easy," Gregor said, looking at his fingers. "But well done."

A car crossed the bridge and pulled up in front of us. A city car. The twin snakes of New Sodom were painted on the door.

A pudgy guy with a pleasant face got out. He had a piece of paper in his hand.

"You the homesteaders?" he said.

"I am. We are," I said, jerking my head toward Turk.

"This is for you, then," the pudgy guy said, and slapped the paper into my hand.

"What is it?" Turk said.

At the top of the paper were the words NOTICE TO CLEAN PREMISES. Below was some legalese telling me that my property was an eyesore and a health hazard, which was true enough, and giving me thirty days to clean the property or lose my claim. Only the word *thirty* had been crossed out, and the word *three* written in above it.

"This is kind of an interesting old form," the guy said. "I've never delivered one like it. You guys are the first homesteaders I ever cited."

"You know," Turk said, "this place doesn't look too different from the other ones around here. Do they all get citations, too?"

"No." The guy shrugged. "There's nobody responsible for most of 'em. Nobody we can find. But you guys are here, and you're responsible."

"Did you cross out this number?" I asked, pointing to the *three*.

"Not me," the guy said. "I just deliver 'em. Rain or shine, weekdays or Sundays."

"But why is it crossed out at all?" I said.

"Everything happens faster these days," the guy said. "Back when this form was printed, a month was probably like three days now."

"We need an extension," I said.

"Oh, you get that down at the department," the guy said. "The thing is, it takes thirty days to process a request. And you've only got three, so—" He shrugged.

Vladimir growled.

The guy lost his grin and backed toward his car.

"Well, good luck," he said, and drove off, bouncing over the potholes and looking back over his shoulder.

"I get the feeling somebody doesn't like us," Turk said.

"Nobody likes you," I said.

"Big joke," Turk said.

"He is right. Nobody likes you," Gregor said, and his guys snickered.

Turk ignored them.

I looked down toward the trees at the river's edge. Some-body was watching this place for sure. Somebody who had enough clout to get a guy from city hall to come out on Sun-day with a carefully modified citation.

"There's only one thing we can do," I said. "We have got to get this place cleaned up. We need Dumpsters. Anybody know anything about getting Dumpsters?"

"They cost hundreds of dollars," Turk said. "I rented one once for an art piece. Wiped out my budget."

I looked at the piles of junk around us. Some of them stood higher than my head.

"We're going to need at least ten big ones," Turk said. "I could maybe afford six."

"I can get the rest," Gregor said.

"Like hell," Turk said. "I don't want to owe you any-thing."

She turned to me. "Want to buy my car?"

"Not even if I had the money," I said.

Gregor was looking at Turk like she'd slapped him, which she pretty much had. "You are a stupid, arrogant girl," he said.

"I don't take favors from anybody," Turk said.

"It is not a favor," Gregor said. "I want to keep my rooms here. That will be hard now that someone knows—that the city knows—"

"This is about those marks, isn't it?" I said.

"Never mind," Gregor said. "You want no favors, and I give you none. But I will buy your worthless car for what-ever price is fair. And please do not think for one moment that I do this for you, stupid gadje cow."

Turk looked down at the ground. "All right, damn it. Three thousand."

"Done," Gregor said. "You will have the money tomorrow. But can all this be cleaned so quickly?"

"It'll have to be, or we lose this place," I said. "Are you guys willing to skip school?"

This was like asking jenti if they wanted to go swimming at the beach. They just didn't do it.

Gregor turned to Vladimir, Ilie, and Constantin. "We will get these Dumpsters, and you will all join me. We will forget school for that day."

"Forget school?" Ilie said.

"All day?" Vladimir said.

"Like gadje?" Constantin said.

"Exactly like gadje," Gregor said. "This is for Burgundy," he added.

Then he walked over to them and put his hand straight out.

"Burgundy," he repeated.

"Burgundy," Ilie said, putting his hand on top of Gregor's.

"Burgundy," Constantin said, slapping his hand down on Ilie's.

"Burgundy," Vladimir said, and put his hand on top of the stack.

"Burgundy, Burgundy, Burgundy, Burgundy," they chanted.

It sounded like they were trying to get served in a wine bar.

Turk held out her car keys.

"Want to take a test-drive?" she said.

"That will not be necessary," Gregor said. "I plan to re-sell your vehicle as soon as I own it."

Turk turned away and headed toward her car.

I followed.

"I'll call as soon as I've got the Dumpsters lined up," I said to Gregor.

"We will be ready," he said.

As we drove back over the bridge, I said, "Just in case you're wondering, I have no idea what that Burgundy stuff was about."

Turk didn't answer. She didn't talk all the way home. I think she was saying good-bye to her car.

16

One thing I did when we got home. I showed my dad the notice.

"Hm," he said when he'd read it. "Looks like you're being set up, all right. You might want to get a lawyer."

"Dad, get a grip," I said. "You're a lawyer, remember?"

"Somebody important really wants you out of there," Dad said like he hadn't heard me. "Funny how everything in life eventually comes down to real estate. It's the damnedest thing."

He gave me back the notice.

"So?" I said.

"So, Leach, Swindol and Twist do a lot of business with the town government," he said. "We're not in a good position to take this case."

"Then how about loaning us ten thousand dollars for some Dumpsters?" I said.

"I'll be in my den," Dad said, and turned away from me.

"Thanks a lot, Uncle Jack," Turk said to Dad's back.

If Dad noticed the dirty looks he was getting from me, Turk, and Mom at dinner, he didn't show it. And he disappeared back into his den as soon as we were done.

Turk went up to her attic and paced back and forth. We could hear her feet stamping up and down the length of the house.

I looked up the numbers of all the Dumpster places in New Sodom and left messages for them to call me the next day. When I was done, I had a message.

Justin had called.

"Need to talk to you," he said when I called back.

"Talk," I said.

"Been thinking about that thing you're doing out in Crossfield," he said. "How's that going?"

"Getting done," I said. "But we've run into trouble."

And I told him about the Dumpsters.

"But we've still got a shot," I said. "Turk's selling her car to Gregor, and with that money we should be able to afford enough of them to get the job done on time."

I made it sound as good as I could. Who knew? Maybe he was calling because he'd decided to help.

That was not the reason.

"Mm-hm," he said when I was done. "Listen, Cody. I've got something to tell you. If you go ahead with this thing, if you turn that old mill into your arts center or anything else, I just don't see how I can go on being friends with you."

"What?" I said. I was sure we had a bad connection.

"I mean it, Cody," Justin said. "You know what that place was."

I didn't say anything for a long time. Then I said, "Yeah. But I also know what it could be."

"No good," Justin said. "It needs to be let alone."

Again, I waited before I spoke.

"How's that going to help?" I finally said.

"Nothing's going to help," Justin said. "That's just the way it is."

"Justin, this isn't about forgetting what happened out there," I said. "It's about going forward. Together."

I was dizzy. The idea of losing Justin was so far out there it didn't seem real. But I knew I hadn't convinced him.

"Cody. One last time. Please quit," Justin said.

"I can't," I blurted out. "Mercy Warrener wouldn't like it."

"Huh?" Justin said. "Mercy Warrener, my ancestor?"

"Yeah, I think so," I said. "She wanted a place where everybody in New Sodom could come together and do things. She didn't call it an arts center. But that was her dream."

"How do you know that?" he asked.

I wanted to tell him. I wanted to get him interested in Mercy Warrener and bring him over to my side. I wanted to tell him about the journal. But a soft voice in my head whispered, *Don't*.

"I can't tell you, exactly," I said.

Now it was Justin who was silent.

"There's an old story in the family about her," he said finally. "She used to say things about how much fun it could be . . . if things were like you say."

"Score," I thought. Jenti take their ancestors very seriously.

"But she sure couldn't have meant to do it in Crossfield," Justin finally said.

"No," I said. "Crossfield's just where it's happening."

My phone went dead.

I thought about calling him back. I thought about calling Ileana and telling her everything we'd said. But what good would that do?

My phone rang. And it was Ileana.

"Justin called me, Cody," she said.

"Yeah," I said.

"He is very upset."

"He's not the only one," I said.

"Cody, I am calling to ask you also. Please give up this idea. For me," Ileana whispered. "I have never asked you for anything, but I am asking you now. Please give up your wonderful idea and let Crossfield be what it is."

"What it is, is ugly and useless," I said.

"Yes," she said. "But there are some things even you cannot change."

I felt sick. I felt scared. It was hard to breathe. I must have known what was coming next.

"I'm sorry," I said. "But I have to push this thing as hard as I can."

"But why?"

"Because . . . because you don't know what you can change unless you try," I said.

"Cody, if you do not do this thing for me, I do not want to see you again. No, that is not true. I do want to see you. But I will not."

I couldn't answer at first. When I thought I had control

of my voice, I said, "I've got a couple of your books. I'll give them back to you at school."

I waited for an answer, but there wasn't one. Just dead air. Then, *click*.

I sat on my bed for a long, long time. And I cycled through more feelings than I usually had in a month. A couple of times, I almost picked up the phone and called Ileana back. All I had to do was agree to drop my stupid idea and everything could go back to the way it was.

Except I couldn't. Not without giving up on Cody Elliot. For the first time, I realized exactly why I was getting myself neck-deep in a swamp full of alligators. Yes, it was for Mercy Warrener, and it was for Ileana. And it might even have been for Turk. But it was definitely because I thought it was the right thing to do. And if I was wrong, I had to find that out for myself.

Life without Ileana and Justin would be one long winter day. A late, cold, gray one, covered with dirty snow. But it was the choice I had made, and I had to live with it.

I went upstairs and scratched on Turk's trapdoor with both hands. When she came to answer it, I said, "I've got to get out of here. Let's go someplace."

"Might as well use my wheels while I've got 'em," she said. "Where do you want to go?"

"Away," I said.

"Dang, Cuz, you sound like you mean it," Turk said. "Let's go."

"Where are you going?" Mom asked as we went out the door.

"Some place Cody told me about," Turk said.

"When will you be back?" Mom asked.

"Yes," Turk said.

"Don't stay out late," Mom said.

Turk's cramped little car grumbled awake and pulled away from the curb. I wanted to be able to do this—to turn a key and drive away from things.

We didn't talk. Turk headed west, the fastest way out of town. When we had left New Sodom behind, she turned onto a side road heading north. A sign said SQUIBNOCKET.

"I've always wanted to see a Squibnocket, haven't you?" Turk said.

"Not much," I said.

The road dipped and twisted through a range of round green hills that got higher as we went north. A strong wind was blowing the clouds south like galloping horses. Or maybe flying jenti. I wondered if Gregor was up there.

"When Mom backstabs me, or gets married or something, I always take off," Turk said. "I drive around till I can stand to go back. Or until I run out of gas money. Doesn't solve anything, but it's better than nothing."

I didn't have anything to say. I just stayed hunched over in the uncomfortable seat.

"Sometimes I just drive around screaming," Turk said. "I scream until my voice is totally shot. Windows up, windows down. Doesn't matter. When you're screaming, people leave you alone."

"Must be nice," I said.

"Look, you don't have to tell me a damn thing," Turk said. "I don't care that much anyway. But if you want to spill your guts about it, go ahead."

"I don't," I said. Then I did.

When I was all spilled out, Turk said, "Know how you feel. I had a friend once. Sucks."

I didn't know if she meant it sucked to lose a friend, or to have one in the first place.

"Know what I did when she backstabbed me?" Turk went on.

"Let me guess," I said. "Did an art project about it with baling wire and old refrigerator parts, and sold if for ten thousand dollars."

"Learned how to drive," Turk said.

We were coming into Squibnocket now. It was one of those towns that haven't changed much in the last few hundred years. A covered bridge led into it, and the biggest building was a stone church with a bell tower.

Turk headed in to the church parking lot. A sign by the driveway said, YOU ARE WELCOME TO OUR PARKING LOT AND TO OUR CHURCH. ST. BIDDULPH'S EPISCOPAL CHURCH.

"I played water polo against these guys," I said.

"Spare me the jock talk," Turk said, and parked the car.

She opened the door and walked around to my side of the car.

"Get out," she said.

"Why?" I said.

Turk shook her head.

"Why did I get all the brains in the family?" she said. "I'm teaching you to drive, Cuz."

Turk was being nice to me. Amazing. But I wasn't in the mood to be amazed. I just sat there.

"Why?" I said.

"Because the way you're feeling right now is the way I feel most of the time," Turk said. "It's nice to have company. Even yours."

I got out and slid in behind the wheel.

When Turk was beside me, she said, "You know gas from clutch?"

I nodded. That was one of the things about driving I already knew.

"Then show me," she said.

I turned the key. The noisy little engine roared behind us.

"Let the clutch out sloooowly," Turk said.

I did, but not slowly enough. There was a loud *bang-thump,* and the car stopped.

I swore.

"No problem," Turk said. "Do it again."

Ten or twenty tries and I was beginning to get the hang of it. And no matter how many times I killed that engine, Turk never lost her cool or said anything sarcastic.

"Okay," she said after I had managed to start and stop the car several times in a row without any mistakes. "That is reverse gear. Put us in it."

I did, and after three tries I got it right. The car began to move backward. Because I was doing it. Slowly, slowly. I didn't want to have any more nasty moments involving the clutch.

I did, and we were facing in a whole new direction.

"Now it starts to get interesting," Turk said. "That is first gear. Put us into first gear and drive us forward. Forward is the opposite of the way we have been going. Turn the wheel so the pointy end of the car goes that way."

I snickered. If Turk was starting to get razor-tongued again, I must be doing all right.

I ground, bashed, and lurched through the three forward gears, over and over, trying to figure out where the point was where you eased into the next one. Around and around that parking lot for more than an hour.

It didn't change anything, but it gave me something else to think about. I had to pay attention to that engine, those pedals, that gearshift. Oh, and the steering wheel. The steering wheel was very important.

Turk kept telling me to do this, try that, change what I was doing to something else, but always in her calm, low voice. She had a good voice, really. I'd never noticed it before.

By the end of the lesson, I could go from a cold stop to third gear without jerking, killing the engine, or making the transmission fall out. Driving around the parking lot at twenty-five or thirty miles an hour felt like a NASCAR rally to me. And really, it was the same thing. Just a lot slower.

"Well, Cuz, I think you've got it," Turk said. "Too bad I have to give up my wheels tomorrow. With a little more practice, you could be a real menace to navigation."

"Thanks, Turk," I said.

"Whatever," she said. "Let me take over now."

We drove back to New Sodom through a night that was so sad and so beautiful I wanted to cry. And the weird thing was, Turk had been right. Nothing had changed. I still had to go back to Vlad knowing that Ileana and Justin wouldn't talk to me. But right now, driving with Turk beside me, I was in a place where it didn't matter quite as much. Maybe something had changed a little after all.

17

I don't know what time it was when I finally got to sleep. All I know is, my phone buzzed way too early.

And it was Gregor.

"Gadje, how did you do this?" he asked. "Even I am a little impressed."

"Do what?" I asked.

"How did you get Dumpsters delivered overnight, and on a Sunday?"

I didn't understand. "Look, Gregor. I told you. We'll try to get the Dumpsters lined up today," I said. "I'll call as soon as the places open."

"You did not do this? Then listen, gadje," Gregor said. "Last night, Vladimir had the duty to guard the mill. He was flying around and he saw a line of headlights coming down the road. Trucks. One after the other, they drove up to the mill and dropped off these large trash bins and went away. There are a dozen, gadje. Call in sick. Get yourself and your lazy cousin over to the mill. We will meet you in an hour."

All of a sudden, I wasn't sleepy anymore. I got up and hauled down Turk's hatch.

"Turk, get up. Major news," I said.

Mom forced us to eat something, which took five minutes. Then we roared across town to Crossfield.

Turk went zipping in and out around the other cars like she was daring them to hit her. I felt like calling my mother to say good-bye and thanks for a good life.

When she jerked up in front of the mill, it was just like Gregor had said. Our place was surrounded by Dumpsters.

Gregor was standing in the entrance with Constantin, Ilie, and Vladimir.

"Did you do this?" Turk snapped, slamming the door of the car.

Gregor shook his head. "Gadje, I had nothing to do with these things and you know it," he said. "If you did not hire them, then we have a true mystery. A boring, stupid mystery, perhaps, but a mystery."

Turk turned to Vladimir.

"Why didn't you grab one of the drivers and ask him who was paying him?" she demanded.

"Why?" Vladimir answered. "I thought surely you and Cody must know."

"Then who the hell did this?" she said. "I don't like this. I don't like it at all."

"Why not?" I said.

"Because it means somebody we don't know is involving themselves with our thing," Turk said. "And we don't know who they are or what they want."

There was nothing on the Dumpsters to tell us who owned them. No phone number on the side.

"I think they want us to clean this place up," I said. "I think we ought to get started."

"Yes," Constantin said. "Let us fill these mysteries up, before they perhaps disappear in a puff of smoke."

He tossed an old machine part into the nearest Dumpster. It clanged like a cracked bell.

"Hey, wait a minute," Turk said.

But the jenti ignored her, and started filling the Dumpster. All the unnamable stuff we'd thrown out of the building went sailing into the big green containers. Things that it would have taken two men to lift, the jenti tossed overhand.

Gregor started singing in high jenti. The other guys joined in on the chorus. I couldn't understand more than a few words of it: *Blood. Swords. Fangs. Death.* And *Burgundy. Burgundy,* over and over.

"Well, come on," I said. "They can't do all the work."

But Turk stalked off with her arms wrapped around herself. We didn't see her again until half the Dumpsters were filled.

She came out of the mill with her cell phone and said, "There are three places in town that rent Dumpsters. I called them all. None of them had a contract to do this. So where the hell are they from? And who the hell is paying for them?"

Gregor said something in jenti. The others laughed.

"What?" Turk said.

"He said, 'She must drink the blood of angels.' I think," I said. "But I don't know what that means, exactly."

"It means you think you are too good to accept good fortune," Gregor said. "Real blood would not be good enough for you. You must have that which does not exist."

"What I want is to know what's going on," Turk said.

"I have an idea," Vladimir said. "Do not go home, gadje girl. Stay here until the mysterious trucks come and remove the containers. Then jump out and capture them all."

"Maybe I will," Turk said.

Constantin and Ilie didn't say anything. They just moved on to the next Dumpster and started filling it.

When we were done, the land around the mill was clean, and there were two empty Dumpsters left over.

We'd beaten the town. Or whoever in town wanted us out of here.

But I didn't feel like a winner. I was totally wasted, worn, and beaten. I had put a lot into this work, trying not to think about Ileana and Justin. I guess it had worked. Right now, I couldn't think about anything except how tired I was.

Even the jenti were wiped.

"Gregor, is this enough?" Constantin panted.

"Yes," Gregor said. Then to Turk he said, "What next, gadje?"

"We need heat and light," I said wearily. "And I don't know yet how we're going to get them."

We all looked toward the sound of a car coming closer. It had an old-fashioned engine that made almost as much noise as Turk's VW, but sounded infinitely classier. A low, elegant car that looked a little like a canoe with headlights pulled up in front.

Only one person in town had a 1923 Hispano-Suiza, and she got out and strode over to us with a swing of her long hair that every boy at Vlad knew. But what was a science teacher doing here?

"So, it is true." Ms. Vukovitch smiled. "There are still pioneers in New Sodom. How's it going with the homestead?"

"We're getting there," I said.

"I tell you why I came," Ms. Vukovitch said. "I hear from somewhere that this old place has the original power plant. Is that so?"

"It sure looks original," I said.

"I have some students. They need a senior project. I hear you're doing this, and I think, 'Vukovitch, maybe restoring an old power plant is hard enough to qualify.' Can I see it?"

"Wait a minute," Turk said. "You do know you're in Crossfield, right?"

Ms. Vukovitch waved her hand and waltzed back to her car. She pulled out a couple of flashlights and handed them to us.

We all went down to the basement and spent the next half hour listening to Ms. Vukovitch practically singing about how great the power plant was.

"My God, what turbines. Built to last a hundred years. And practically mint condition. Old, but also very good. Of course, the wiring needs to be brought up to code. But any idiot can do that. In fact, I have just the idiots. We get this system working again, modernize lighting, throw in redesign of heating plant to make a green building out of it— worth an A or two, maybe. What do you think? When can we start?"

"Who's going to pay for it?" Turk asked.

"The richest school in the state," Ms. Vukovitch said. "I've got a huge budget for senior projects."

"What's your budget for Dumpsters like?" Turk asked.

"What?" Ms. Vukovitch sounded confused.

"Never mind," Turk said. "You can start as soon as you want."

"Tomorrow, then," Ms. Vukovitch said. "Me and a few of the boys will come out and see what we need to get started."

The sun was setting when we came back out. Ms. Vukovitch's Hispano-Suiza bounded away toward the river. The jenti spread their wings and flapped them slowly, flying away from town, except for Ilie, who stationed himself on the roof.

Turk and I got into her car.

"Do you believe that story Vukovitch gave us about the school paying for everything? I sure as hell don't," Turk said.

"Why not?" I said. "Vlad has plenty of money."

"Maybe. But why did she just show up, two seconds after school was over for the day? How did she know anybody was going to be here? Why is she offering us help at all? This is Crossfield, damn it. The Great Unmentionable."

"Yeah," I said. If I hadn't been so tired and sad, I might have thought of that myself.

"I feel like I'm part of somebody else's game," Turk said. "But what game, and what are the rules? And what's the prize?"

I looked back over my shoulder at our mill and its

necklace of Dumpsters. It looked a little like Stonehenge, or what I thought Stonehenge might look like if it had been made of large trash containers.

It was a mystery, all right. But maybe it meant somebody was on our side.

18

Tuesday, when I saw Ileana at Vlad, I handed back the books she'd loaned me.

"Thanks," I said. "I really liked them."

"You are welcome. I am glad," she said, and took them and went on down the hall.

I could hear the Rustle starting around me.

Cody Elliot and our princess are fighting.

What is it about? The cousin?

No. This is something else. But the cousin is part of it.

And Justin Warrener?

He is part of it.

Okay, I was imagining the words. But it was real.

Rustle, Rustle, Rustle.

I didn't see Justin. He was absent, which was strange because he was never absent. But it was just as well. Parting from Ileana was hard enough.

I hurt like I had never hurt before. And the day sped by like a rock rolling uphill.

One good thing did happen. After school, we met the guy from code enforcement out at the mill.

Turk and I were waiting when he drove up.

He took a look around and said, "Man, how did you kids do all this?"

"Never mind," Turk said. "We did it. So certify us, or whatever you do."

"Well," the guy said, "I'm not sure I can. The Dumpsters are still here."

I raised my hand over my head.

From up on the roof of the mill where they had been lying, Gregor, Constantin, Ilie, and Vladimir came spiraling down. Ms. Vukovitch, who had been watching from inside the mill, came out with six big seniors.

Vladimir and Ilie leaned on the guy's car. Gregor came over to us.

"Everything is fine now, yes?" he asked me.

"He thinks the Dumpsters might be a problem," I said. "But he's not sure."

"Oh, I can let it go for now," he said. "Let the guys downtown sort it out."

"It is sorted out," Gregor said. "It is sorted into the Dumpsters, yes? What more is there to sort?"

"Yeah, maybe you're right," the guy said. "I'll just sign off on it. I mean, you're not going to keep the Dumpsters, are you?"

"Not even one," I said.

The guy scribbled his name on a certificate of compliance that looked like it had been printed in 1890, and got out of there.

We all waved.

"Score one for the homesteaders," Ms. Vukovitch said. "Back to work, guys."

The Dumpsters disappeared that night.

So the settlers had stood off two attacks now, and I should have at least been happy about that, right? Right. But then, the next day, I saw Justin and got my guts kicked in again.

He was walking down the hall talking to Ileana. His right hand was bandaged.

As they passed me, I heard him say, "Yeah. Burned it over the weekend, camping. With the Mercians. Stupid of me."

I was pretty sure those words were for me. And I was even more sure that they were a lie. Justin camping was about as likely as me singing grand opera. And I had a sickening feeling that I knew exactly where, and how, he'd really burned his hand.

"You're right," I said to his back. "You don't know how stupid."

Justin didn't seem to have heard.

At least the work on the mill was going ahead. Ms. Vukovitch and her seniors treated the old turbines and generator like they were a work of art they were restoring. And when they had them running again, they replaced every rat-eaten, rubber-covered, hundred-year-old conduit in the place with new wiring, and ran extra lines for all the new features.

"What's down in that generator room was built to run big, inefficient machines," Ms. Vukovitch told me and Turk when we went by to help. "We're going to have extra power to burn."

They modernized the heating system, too. The old place would never be a very green building, but from somewhere came triple-paned windows and insulation for the attics.

Meanwhile, Turk, Gregor, Ilie, Constantin, Vladimir, and yours truly did all kinds of stuff. My hands stung from feathery little fiberglass cuts. My eyes were red from sawdust and cleaning chemicals. I was wiped when I fell into bed each night, and I barely thought about my schoolwork. But the building was coming to life under our hands. I clung to that.

But homework was homework, whether I did it or not.

Friday night, when I would normally have been doing something with Ileana, I was up in my room staring at the science assignment that was due last Wednesday. It was a Vlad classic.

> *Compare and contrast the anatomy of the modern cod with that of the bony fishes of the late Devonian period. In part one of your answer, confine yourself to a detailed analysis of jaws and skulls. In the second part, speculate intelligently on what might be deduced about the soft anatomy of the Devonian species from the modern examples. 2,500 words.*

I knew what the words meant. But as far as doing anything about them went, they might as well have been in Babylonian.

I couldn't stop thinking about Justin and Ileana. Literally could not stop. Even when I was working at the mill, my mind kept running over what they had said, remembering

Justin's burned hand. The world was a gray, hollow place without them, and there was nothing that would help that. Plus, they'd always been there to help me with the impossible assignments that made Vlad the toughest school in the known universe. And now there was no one.

I was giving serious thought to jumping out the window when there was a scratching at my door.

"Beat it, Turk," I said.

But the scratching went on.

Finally, I got up from my desk, went over to my door, and jerked it open.

"Leave me alone," I said.

Turk was standing there with two hot mochas in one hand and her laptop under her arm.

"Want to do homework?" she said.

"No," I said.

"Good," she said. "Me neither." And she came in.

She looked at my science assignment.

"Devonian fishes and cod?" she said. "That's totally lame. It should be a comparison of Devonian fishes and sharks. Then you might have something valid. Well, what have you got so far?"

" 'The,' " I said. "And thanks for the mocha, by the way."

"Whatever," Turk said. "Talk fish to me."

And it was weird, but talking to Turk worked. She wasn't even in the same class I was, but she knew what questions to ask. And by answering them, I got the framework of my answer. By the time we were done, I had five pages of notes. I could write that essay in a couple of hours now.

To celebrate, we went down to the espresso machine and made two more mochas.

"I got to tell you, Turk," I said. "That was a huge help."

"What else you got?" she said.

I had a rewrite of a history assignment, I had two lessons in high jenti, I had a math assignment that could have had Einstein reaching for his cheat sheet, and I had a few other things.

"Let's take a look at 'em," Turk said.

By midnight, we had the math knocked off, the history thing redone, and everything else except the high jenti, which Turk didn't know any more about than I did. It was amazing to work with her. Her mind was like a machine, slicing the assignments into doable chunks, and showing me how to fit them back together. By the time we were done, I felt like there was nothing I had to learn that I couldn't handle—as long as I had Turk to help me.

"Want to kick back?" I said when we were finished.

"What've you got in mind?" she said.

"Something wild and crazy," I said. "Like watching an old movie, maybe."

"Something with vampires," Turk said.

Mom and Dad were already in bed, so we took over the watching room. This was the name Mom had given to the room downstairs where she and Dad curled up with their movies after Dad had brought in our gigantic new flatscreen.

Turk picked out something with a title like *Dracula's Third Cousin*. It was a typical vampire flick. Castles, dark and stormy nights, and Count Casimir, a tall, dark guy with an English accent who went around sucking blood until somebody put a stake in his heart after about an hour and a half.

I'd seen this movie five or six times. It was a joke. But

tonight, it wasn't funny. Somehow, the stupid script and the hammy acting were real in a way they'd never been. Not scary real, sad real. And damn it, when the vampire nailed his third victim, I started to cry.

That was weird enough. But what happened next was even weirder. Turk put her arms around me.

"Hey," she said. "Hey, go ahead, stupid. It's about time."

And I did.

When I was wiping my nose and the movie credits were rolling up the screen, I felt better, the way you do, and I hugged Turk back.

"Easy," she said. "I can't take too much touchy-feely family stuff."

"Yeah," I said, grinning, my voice shaky. "Why are you being so nice to me, anyway?"

"I feel sorry for you," Turk said. "I figure you're finding out what I've known since I was six. People always leave you."

"No, they don't," I said. "A lot of people hang together forever."

"How many friends from California are still in your life?" Turk said.

"I still get e-mail from some of them," I said.

"When was the last time?" Turk asked.

I couldn't remember.

"A few months," I said. "I guess. But my parents. I mean, a lot of people. People in New Sodom. Jenti stick together like they've got Velcro on their wings."

"Not so much," Turk said. "A lot of the people you think are tight with each other aren't. It just looks that way. From the outside."

"You still haven't said anything about my mom and dad," I said.

"How long have they been together?" Turk said. "Eighteen, twenty years? It's a long time, Cuz, but it ain't forever. Forever hasn't happened yet. And when it does, there'll still be one of them left, alone."

"You sure know how to cheer a guy up," I said.

"It's just the way it is." Turk shrugged. "And the sooner you get it, the sooner you can stop worrying about it."

"Like you don't worry about it?" I said.

"I don't," Turk said. "I've figured out how to deal."

"Yeah, how?" I said.

"Always leave first," Turk said.

I didn't think I believed her. Actually, I didn't think she believed herself. If she did, why was she being so good to me when I needed it so badly? But if there was one thing I'd learned about Turk, it was that she wasn't easy to figure out.

19

I'm thinking we want to open on Halloween," Turk said.

She was standing in the big open space on the first floor, gnawing delicately on her thumbnail. Above her head were a couple of seniors, wings spread, working on the ceiling fixtures.

"Good choice. Halloween's on Saturday this year," I said. "But what'll we open with?"

Turk gave me a disgusted look.

"My show. Duh," she said. "It's going to be right here."

"Oh. Yes. I meant, 'What else will we open with besides your magnificent creations?'" I said. "You know—like the basic idea of the whole thing?"

"Yeah. You're right," Turk said, brushing her chin with

her sleeve. "We ought to hit up every community arts organization in New Sodom and offer them space here that night. It's time to start getting political."

"Political how?" I said.

"Come on, Cuz. Do I have to explain everything on the planet to you? We need people on our side. And the best way to get that is to give them something first. We offer them a venue. They come in and do their thing. Their friends come, and pretty soon they're our friends, too. That's when this thing will really take off."

"In case you haven't noticed, it's political already," I said. "Political enough that my best friend and my girl broke up with me. Political enough that whatever friends we do have have had to help us in secret. The only jenti who've worked here up front are Gregor and his gang, and Ms. Vukovitch and her guys. And all of them are from Europe. The Crossfield thing doesn't mean as much to them. And just for the record, no gadje at all are showing up to help."

"That's what I mean. They need to get past that," Turk said.

I had deep reservations about Turk being able to make friends with anybody. But even if she could, we only had about a month. And whatever arts groups we had in New Sodom probably weren't sitting around with ready-to-run programs in their pockets. Say somebody wanted to put on a play: it would have to be selected, cast, and rehearsed. Same thing for a concert. Even I knew it wasn't going to be easy.

But that was the same day they finished the wiring, and Ms. Vukovitch purred, "Okay, guys, time to test the whole system. Turn on every light in the place."

When we did that, the mill changed into something it had never been before. It glowed. The walls were deep, warm red; the scarred old floors had a soft yellow gleam.

The little wigwam we'd built in the lobby looked shabby and out of place, but it seemed to be saying, "Remember how all this started."

All of us—me, Turk, Ms. Vukovitch and her boys, and Gregor and his guys—went from room to room admiring what we'd done.

"Great job," Turk said at last. "Gregor, you and your thugs can clean up my messes anytime."

"Pah," Gregor said. "We did none of it for you. But you are right. We have made this into something very acceptable with our work."

"Acceptable, my left wing," Ms. Vukovitch said. "It is a palace."

"Let's go outside," I said.

It was hard to believe, but the old place was nearly ready for its new life.

The sun was down. A chilly wind was coming up from the river. Crossfield looked as dark and lost as always. But the lights glowing behind our windows fell on the barren ground in every direction. The crisscross patterns of the windows looked like the narrow stone paths that held down the past all around us. But these were not part of the past. These were the future, if we could make it happen.

"How's this, Mercy?" I wondered aloud. "Is this good enough? Anyway, we're almost ready."

It was a palace. A palace of light.

20

The next day, Turk and I visited the school library. Ms. Shadwell showed us a plastic-covered notebook that had the names and addresses of all the community organizations in it. There were the Society for the Preservation of Oak Trees, the Friends of the Gomorrah River, the Association of King Charles Spaniel Fanciers, the John Keats Chapter of the Federation of Romantic Poets, Post 147 of the Massachusetts Colonial Historical Association—it went on for two hundred pages. But only a few were arts groups.

Turk and I made a list of all the ones that sounded even remotely right, and started calling their presidents. Every one of them, from the New Sodom Light Opera Guild to the Daughters of Terpsichore Classical Dance Circle, turned us down.

"How very kind of you to think of us in this way," the president of the Thalian Confederation for Oral Recitation told me. "We do wish you the best of luck with your project. But it isn't quite right for us."

"What a lovely idea," said the president of the Aeolian Society for the Propagation of Sixteenth-Century Wind Music. "But I doubt that the acoustics of an old mill would favor our efforts."

And the president of the Friends of Folkloric Musical Performance told Turk, "We couldn't possibly appear in a venue that was originally a site of labor exploitation."

The first week of October ticked by. The second. Nobody wanted to be part of the opening.

Turk got busy with her show. She spent all her afternoons out at the mill hanging her work.

"Hell, who cares if they don't show?" she said. "I'm going to have my art up. That's what matters."

I was pretty sure Turk was self-involved enough not to care if anybody else used the center or not. She was probably enjoying the picture of herself as someone too special for New Sodom. I could imagine her standing alone in the gallery on the main floor, just her and her art and her inflatable *Scream*.

But I did care. In between missing Justin and wishing I were with Ileana, I worried about an opening night where nobody came. I wanted a night where people were falling out the windows because it was so crowded inside, with everybody saying, "How come no one ever did this before?" At the very least, I wanted it to be important enough that Justin and Ileana would know that I had been right.

If I was right.

I kept thinking about an old joke Dad told me he used to

see on signs plastered around his college campus: TOMOR-ROW HAS BEEN CANCELED DUE TO LACK OF INTEREST. It looked like we might be on our way to being that joke.

Then I got a clue as to just how very interested some people were.

It was Columbus Day. In Massachusetts, that's a day off from school. Turk and I were celebrating by trying to catch up on our homework. I read English while she worked through her math, science, and history.

Meanwhile, it was a beautiful day outside. All the leaves were beginning to turn, and some of the trees were like crowns of red and gold already. The air was warm, and bright with that special light that says, "Enjoy this. It won't last long" and makes everything stand out sharp and clear.

By four o'clock, the shadows were getting thick under the trees in the backyard, and the last hour of daylight was starting to slide toward evening. I had spent hours slogging through a sludge of nineteenth-century poetry, most of it written to girls with names like Annabelle and Maude, poems that seemed as thick on the page as the shadows outside, and not anywhere near as beautiful. And they made me think about Ileana more, which was not the best thing to have happen.

So when Turk stuck her head in my bedroom door and said, "Let's blow up this place and get out of here," I was ready, even though I had about a hundred more pages of Annabelles to go.

We got into her car and drove down to the Screaming Bean.

The Screaming Bean was a downtown coffee joint. There was a life-sized version of *The Scream*, just like Turk's, on the front door, and across the bottom, in words cut from old magazines, it said, "WHAT do you mean there's no COF-fee?!?!?!?!"

"Hey, look. Your friend's here," I said.

"*The Scream* is everywhere," Turk sighed. "It's become a cliché. You don't see inflatable Rothkos, do you?"

Whatever that meant.

Anyway, I pushed open the door and in we went.

Inside, it was a Turk kind of place. Dark walls with things on them that I guess were art, because they had price tags. There were tables and chairs that looked like they'd been salvaged from the *Titanic*. The backs of the chairs and the tops of the tables had been covered with photographs and paintings under heavy coats of thick, clear lacquer. All of these things had been clipped from magazines, and all of them showed terrible things happening to the people in them. On every chair and table were the same words: WHAT DO YOU MEAN THERE'S NO COFFEE?!?!?!?!

The customers were mostly kids and mostly gadje, though there were a few jenti kids in one corner. Whichever they were, they all looked like Turk. I wondered if she'd found her own kind here.

It was pretty cool, actually. There was a little stage in one corner with a sign behind it that said POETRY SLAM 7 PM FRIDAY. Next to it was a handmade poster for the Sixty-Minute Shakespeare Theater Company.

Some kind of techno-pop music was playing over the sound system.

I got us a couple of cups of coffee and a sweet roll.

"I kind of like this place," Turk said. "Not great, but it tries. And the coffee would strip paint."

"When do you even find time to come here?" I asked.

"Whenever I want to," Turk said.

"Is any of this stuff yours?" I asked.

Turk pointed one black fingernail straight up.

Over our heads was a paper snake like the one in Turk's attic, but gigantic. It looped and coiled all over the ceiling. Huge paper wings stuck out from its sides and drooped down. Its jaw hung open to show a double row of fangs.

It was impressive, but there was something weird about it. It didn't really look like a snake. The head was wrong. On the other hand, why not? Flying snakes are rare, and their heads might look a little odd. But what was it about the face that bothered me?

Then I realized what it was.

"It's Gregor," I said.

Turk grinned.

"Not bad, Cuz," she said. "Hanging out with me has definitely made you smarter."

"Does he know?" I asked.

"Like I'm going to tell him," Turk said. "It's a private joke."

"Why did you do it?" I asked.

Turk shrugged. "You've got a point," she said. "It should have been a pig. Or a jackass."

"He's been a lot of help," I pointed out. "Him and his guys. Without them, we'd be nowhere near ready to open."

"Give me a break, Cuz. You don't like him any better than I do," Turk said.

She reached up under her shades and wiped away an invisible tear.

"Oh, Cody," she said. "How noble you are. How fair-minded. You shame me."

"As if anybody could shame you," I said.

We drank our coffee and took turns eating the sweet roll.

Outside, the golden light was gone. The shadows spread across the window.

I looked at the kids sitting around us. A couple of them were typing away on laptops. A few others were reading or sketching.

"Hey," I said. "Maybe we ought to try asking these guys."

"Asking them what?" Turk said.

"If they'd like to be part of the opening," I said.

"Nooo," Turk said slowly.

"Why not? Especially since we haven't got anybody else," I said.

"Because they're nobodies," Turk said. "And nobodies can't help us."

"You know what, Turk?" I said. "You don't want any help anyway. Gregor helps, Ms. Vukovitch helps. Somebody with a mess of Dumpsters helps. You sneer at them, or you get all paranoid. Maybe what you really want is a bunch of people who can't help."

Turk snorted. "Don't try to figure me out, Cuz. You're not smart enough."

I didn't want to get into a fight with her, so I looked up at the ceiling. At that big Gregor dragon-snake thing.

And then I proved Turk was wrong. Because I had figured out something about her that she would have killed me for knowing. She had picked where we sat. Our table was right under the snake, where the wings joined the body.

Rest beneath the shadow of my wings.

Gregor and Turk? The idea hit me like a splash of icy water.

Gregor and Turk. And Turk would rather die of lockjaw than ever admit it to anybody.

"What?" Turk said. "Your face is all stupid-looking."

"Nothing," I said. "You wouldn't believe me if I told you."

My phone buzzed.

"Mr. Cody Elliot?"

A man's voice. Kind of old-sounding.

"Yes," I said.

"I represent the New Sodom Federation for the Arts. We are interested in exhibiting at your venue. I would like to discuss matters of fees, available space, that sort of thing. Might we meet in perhaps an hour?"

"The New Sodom Federation for the Arts?" I said. "Who are you, exactly?" I was sure they hadn't been in Ms. Shadwell's binder.

"We include about forty arts and performance groups in the area," the voice said. "Not all of them are in New Sodom, in spite of the name. I hope that's not a problem."

"Uh—no," I said. "Certainly not. Where would you like to meet?"

The voice gave me an address in Squibnocket.

"I'll be there," I said, and snapped the phone shut.

"I've got to get to Squibnocket," I said. "Can you take me?"

"You want another driving lesson?" Turk said.

I told her what the voice had said.

"Whoa," she said. "Who are these guys? And how do they just show up out of the blue? I don't like it, Cuz. I do not like it."

"Well then, you'd better come along to the meeting," I said. "Make sure I'm all right."

"I'll make sure you don't give away the farm," Turk said. "If these guys are talking about paying for space, there'd better be somebody there who knows what space is worth. And that's me. No offense, Cuz, but you're too much of a kid for a guy like this to take seriously."

"You're a kid," I said.

"I'm a pro," Turk said. "And this is the kind of work I do. Come on."

After we reached Squibnocket, we ended up at the edge of the business district. The address was in a neighborhood that was mostly warehouses and small industrial businesses in long one-story buildings that faced away from the street. It was quiet now, because everything was closed for the night.

"This can't be right," I said.

"Sure it can," Turk said. "This is just the kind of place to get a cheap rent." And she drove down the alley that ran between two of the long lines of low buildings.

We stopped in front of the last door.

It was an ordinary glass door next to an ordinary shop window. There was a sign over the door that said COMPRE-HENSIVE INSURANCE. But the space inside the shop was empty.

"What is this?" I said. "I must have got the address wrong."

Then the door swung open and a dapper little gray-haired man beckoned to me. I was pretty sure he was jenti.

"Mr. Elliot? Please come in," he said.

It was the voice I'd heard on the phone.

Turk and I got out of the car.

"Oh, I'd assumed you'd come by yourself," he said.

"We're partners," Turk said. "Co-owners. I'm Turk Stone, the artist."

"Oh. Well, please come in," the little man said. He didn't sound happy.

He held the door open and we passed by him and into the shop. Then the door slammed behind us, and a gloved fist smashed the side of my head.

"Wait, no! He's marked," the little man said. "And leave the girl—"

"Arthur, shut up," another voice said.

I saw figures wearing black hoods blocking the door, grabbing Turk, grabbing me.

And then the blows came, and kept coming until I couldn't feel them anymore.

21

I woke up the next morning, but I didn't want to.

My eyes fluttered open, then closed, then open again. I raised my head, looked around, but nothing made sense. I didn't know where I was.

Turk cursed. Her voice was rough, as if she'd been screaming. A lot.

Mom came over and took my hand.

"Cody," she said, and started to cry.

"Where are we?" I asked.

It really hurt to talk.

"Oh, thank God," Dad said.

"Hospital, Cuz," Turk said. "They let us go when they were done with you."

"Turk drove you here," Mom said.

"I called the cops as soon as I was away from that place," Turk said. "But they haven't found anybody, of course."

"What happened?" I asked.

"There were six of them, not counting that little bastard who let us in," Turk said. "One of them picked me up like I was nothing. Put some kind of a sack over my head and held me while they did you. I screamed, for all the good that did. Then they threw you out, shoved me in the car, and drove off. I called your dad and asked where to take you."

Turk's face was like a map of the world, all different colors. They'd knocked her around, too. I couldn't guess how I must look.

I hurt everywhere, and I was afraid to try to move.

"How bad am I?" I asked.

"The doctor says they were very careful with you," Dad said. "Nothing broken. Nothing permanent."

Then he sobbed, and stopped himself.

Mom cursed. An amazing curse. A jenti couldn't have done it better.

"Cody," Dad said, trying to keep from crying, "what are you involved with? What the hell is going on?"

"I don't know," I said.

There was a sound in the hallway, and we all looked toward the door.

"May I come in?" Gregor asked.

"Yeah," Turk said.

But he didn't move until I croaked, "Okay."

Then he walked over to us stiffly.

"Mom, Dad, this is Gregor Dimitru. Gregor, these are my folks, Jack and Beth Elliot."

Gregor bowed to my mother. Then he took Dad's hand. "Rest beneath the shadow of my wings," he said.

His accent was thick the way it was when he was angry.

"You are all right?" he asked Turk. "No one told me you were hurt. No one—"

"What do you want?" Turk asked.

"This morning I received a phone call," Gregor said. "It was in class, so I did not answer it. But I do not get phone calls, so I listen when class is over. Someone I do not know tells me you are here, and I come."

"And why would someone tell you?" Dad asked in his lawyer voice.

"Because I help with the center of arts," Gregor said. "And because of what I am."

"And what exactly would that be?" Dad asked.

"I am a noble of Burgundy," Gregor said. "Of the Dimitru-Dracul line. Do you know what that means, sir?"

"Not yet. But you're going to tell me," Dad said.

Gregor wasn't intimidated.

"It means that I have power among the jenti. This attack on these two was a warning to them, and an insult to me. A very great insult."

"Back up," Dad said. "Why would anyone do this? What's really going on?"

But just then Ileana and Justin came in.

Ileana looked like a queen. A very serious queen. She looked around the room, took us all in, then came over to my bed and said, "Dear Cody, I am so—"

But Gregor had leapt on Justin and was holding him against the wall.

"I am going to buy myself a dog, Warrener. A large dog.

Then I am going to tear out your throat and feed it to him. The rest of you, I will send to your friends. That will be my answer to the Mercians."

"Let go of him, Gregor," Ileana said.

Justin didn't even try to fight back.

"Go ahead," he said. "I deserve it."

"What?" I croaked.

A couple of nurses came in to tell us to shut up.

Dad went over and closed the door to the room.

"Okay," he said. "I'm a lawyer, and that's my son in that bed. And I want answers now." He crossed his arms and leaned against the door. "Cody, Turk, I'll start with you. What's going on in Crossfield?"

Neither of us could talk for long. We took turns filling Dad in on the mill, the break-in, the scratches over the storeroom. I told him about the Dumpsters. Turk covered the help from Ms. Vukovitch.

"Thank you," Dad said. "Now, which of the three of you can explain most quickly why my son and my niece have been beaten?"

"He can," Gregor said, looking at Justin. "Ask him now, while he still has his throat."

"Mr. Elliot, I'll tell you everything I can," Justin said. "But I don't know all of it. I'm new in the Mercians. All I know for sure is they don't want the arts center to open. Partly it's because it's in Crossfield. But I'm pretty sure there's more to it than that. There has to be. Otherwise, this would never have happened."

"And what exactly is a Mercian, Mr. Warrener?" Dad said.

"A kind of organization some of the old English jenti

166

families belong to," Justin said. "You have to be invited to join. They asked me just a couple of months ago."

"Congratulations," Dad said. "Now, apart from beating teenaged children into unconsciousness, what are the activities of this group?"

"It's just supposed to keep an eye on things," Justin said. "Make sure nothing bad happens in New Sodom. Back in the old days, they were the jenti militia. Now it's more of a social group. Like the Masons."

"So this social group that seeks the betterment of New Sodom decided that an arts center represented a threat to the community, and that the way to prevent its opening was to put my son and my niece in fear for their lives, is that correct?" Dad said.

You could tell he was furious by how calm he was.

"It's not really like that," Justin said.

"Cody didn't put himself in that bed," Dad said. "And Turk did not do that to her own face. Which leads to the question, what did you do to help bring this about? Were you one of the ones who beat them up?"

"Of course not," Justin said. "But what I did was just as bad."

"So you knew it was going to happen," Dad said.

"No," Justin said. "But—somebody—asked me for Cody's cell number, and I gave it to them. I didn't know why they wanted it."

"Still, you could probably guess it wasn't to invite him to your next meeting," Dad said. "Unless that was one of your meetings, of course."

I didn't feel sorry for Justin, but I could see he was practically falling apart.

"Tell him the rest, Warrener," Gregor said. "You are leaving out the best part."

"You tell him," Justin said, and hung his head.

"I will explain it," Ileana said. "I am the highest here."

She was so tiny and so beautiful, and she was acting like I wasn't even there.

"Mr. Elliot, you know that there are old hatreds between the jenti and the gadje of New Sodom," Ileana said. "What you do not know about, because we do not speak of them to outsiders, is the hates between the jenti, and how old they are. Justin descends from a line that goes back to the Kingdom of Mercia, which was in England more than a thousand years ago before it disappeared. Gregor and I descend from the Burgundians, who disappeared on the Russian steppes five hundred years before the Mercians were lost to history.

"The last Burgundians made their way to Mercia, looking for refuge. It was refused them, and they were forced to leave, and take their chances among the gadje of Europe. No one knows why anymore, but this cruelty the Burgundians have never forgotten.

"Then, over a hundred years ago, the Burgundian jenti began to arrive in America, along with other central Europeans. We found New Sodom, a place where gadje and Mercians were living together in peace, if not in love, and we stayed. This time, the Mercians could not drive us out, because we came in such numbers. And we did not try to force them to leave, because we feared they and the gadje would combine against us."

"Fascinating, Ileana," Dad said. "But what does it have to do with anything?"

"It has this to do with anything, Mr. Elliot," Gregor said. "I have put that mill in Crossfield under my protection. The Mercians know this, and they wish to prevent it."

"Why?" Dad shouted. "What is so damned important that my son is lying beaten half to death? What matters that much?"

"That I do not know," Gregor said. "But there is something more than an old grudge at work here. Some deeper thing."

"Well?" Dad asked Justin.

"I don't know what it is," Justin said.

"Do you think you might be able to find out?" Dad said slowly, trying to hold his anger in.

"Nobody's going to tell me if I just ask 'em," Justin said.

"Let me tell you something without your asking," Gregor said. "You Mercians crossed a line last night. You beat a marked gadje. That is an unforgivable insult to our princess. To all of us. If you want war, you shall have it."

"No," Ileana said. "I forbid that. It is true what the Mercians did was despicable. But we must not go to war over it."

"What mark are you talking about?" Dad said.

"Ileana marked me the first day of school last year," I said. "To protect me. It's supposed to mean no jenti can touch me."

"And now we see how much it means to the Mercians," Gregor said. "That was your mark, my princess. If you think this is not worth fighting over, what do you propose to do instead?"

Ileana bit her lip. Then she said, "Justin, you must tell the Mercians that my mother, the Queen of the Burgundians, demands a meeting with them."

"Ah, a meeting." Gregor sneered. "That will solve everything."

"I'll tell them," Justin said.

"Princess, my people will not be satisfied with a meeting," Gregor said.

"Your people are my people, Gregor," Ileana said. "We are all my mother's subjects."

"We will see whom they follow now," Gregor said.

"Do nothing, Gregor," Ileana commanded. "We will settle this."

Gregor came over to my bed.

"I will avenge this crime," he said. But he was looking at Turk when he said it.

She looked away, and Gregor left.

"Justin, we must go," Ileana said.

"Right," Justin said. "I'll set things up."

"So that's it, then?" Dad said. "You kids just walk away and go on playing your jenti games?"

"Mr. Elliot, it is no game," Ileana said. "There is great danger in New Sodom now. More than there has been in three hundred years. And we do not know why. We must find out before there is blood and fire."

Then she looked at me. There were tears in her eyes. Her hand reached itself out, but she snatched it back.

"Come," she said, and left, with Justin behind her.

"Cody, can you, for God's sake, explain any of this?" Dad said.

I realized then how little my dad really knew about my life in New Sodom. About his own life here, really. I'd have to teach him fast.

"Let's start with marking," I said.

22

I came home from the hospital two days later. Mom set me up on the couch in the living room, where she could keep an eye on me and bring me stuff.

I didn't do much except lie around and wish I were dead. Inside and out, I'd been so thoroughly beaten up that there was no place left that didn't hurt.

But things can always get worse, and the day after I came home from the hospital, they did.

It was on the front page of the New Sodom *Intelligencer,* the local paper:

† † †

TOWN COUNCIL TAKES NEW SODOM OUT
OF 17TH CENTURY

In a place as old as New Sodom, some funny old laws can turn up. One that has recently come to light involves Crossfield.

Crossfield? Yes, that Crossfield.

It seems that, back in the day, some long-gone town council thought it would be a good idea to let anyone who wanted it claim abandoned land there. In the words of the act, "When it shall hap that a farm or steading of any sort shall be left untenanted for the time of three yeares, and no owner be writ down in the towne records, whoso shall tenant it and build thereon a cabin or a wigwam, and plante corne, and dwell for seven yeares upon it, shall have possession of said farm or steading so long as it shall please him. To keep or to sell, to leave unto descendants, and to do all things that may be done with a farm or steading."

Now, before you rush over to Crossfield and start throwing up your wigwam, there are two things you need to know: (1) some kids actually tried it, staking out the old Simmons Mill just as though it were still 1676; (2) when the town council found out about it, they repealed the act.

"It was just one of those crazy things that happen," said town council member Watson Waters. "That and some half-bright kids who thought they could get away with something."

But why would kids want to take over an abandoned mill anyway?

"We heard that they wanted to start some kind of a half-baked arts center over there, even though no arts group in New Sodom wanted anything to do with it," Waters said. "We're not sure what they were really up to."

In any case, with the kids gone, the act repealed, and police tape around the outside of the Simmons Mill, it's pretty clear that whatever it was won't be happening anytime soon.

"Can they do that, Dad?" I said. "Can they just take it away from us?"

We were sitting around the living room that morning, me, Mom, Dad, and Turk. I was doing a lot better and was dressed to go out, even though I wasn't going back to Vlad yet.

"It depends," Dad said. "Certainly there's an argument to be made that whatever changes they made to the act don't apply to the Simmons Mill. But ultimately, the town can claim eminent domain, and probably make it stick. On the other hand, there's such a thing as just compensation. If they take something away from you, they have to pay you the fair market value. On the other hand, you've staked your claim but you haven't completed the seven-year term that would make it yours. So they could probably claim they didn't owe you anything. It's a very interesting question."

"Interesting enough to take to court?" Turk asked.

"No," Dad said.

"Ah, yes," Turk said. "Leach, Swindol and Twist. Complications with the town. Wouldn't want those."

"Turk, do you really think it would be a good idea to go ahead with this?" Dad asked.

"Yes," I said.

"Well, that's a point of view," Dad said. "Personally, I don't give a damn whether New Sodom has an arts center or not. My only concern is that you two not get hurt in some damn fool jenti war. If those overeducated idiots want to fight about who did what to whom back in the Middle Ages, let 'em. But they'd better leave us alone."

"I can't believe you just said that," I said.

"Neither can I," Mom said. "Anyway, Jack, what kind of safety can we have if our neighbors are killing each other?"

Turk didn't say anything.

"In any case, there's nothing I can do that will make this situation better," Dad said.

And he got up and went to work.

Turk went to school. I could tell she was furious with Dad.

That was a strange day. The house was absolutely quiet. We were waiting for something, and we didn't know what.

Turk came home, and brought me some assignments.

"Weird stuff at Vlad," she said. "I don't know what. Feels bad."

"Did you see Gregor or Ileana?" I asked.

"She was around, he wasn't," Turk said. "And your buddy Justin was following her around like a lost puppy. You know, jenti are jerks. All of 'em."

And she went upstairs.

It wasn't half an hour later that the doorbell rang. Just because I felt like I could do it, I walked all the way from the couch to the door, and opened it.

Gregor nodded to me.

"Have I your permission to enter?" he said in high jenti.

"Rest beneath the shadow of my wings," I said, and let him in.

He gave a half smirk at my words and said, "May I see your cousin?"

Now, here was a challenge. Going upstairs. What an adventure.

I hobbled up the first few steps.

"May I help you?" Gregor said.

"I got it," I said. "Thanks."

Turk's ladder was down.

"Turk, you have company," I said. "Gregor."

"What do you want?" came Turk's voice.

And Gregor went up.

Up went the ladder.

I went back downstairs.

It was strange to think of Gregor in my house. We never saw each other except at Vlad and the mill.

From the living room, Mom and I listened to the sounds of their voices.

"It sounds like they're fighting," Mom said.

"That's what they do," I said.

After a few minutes, Turk called down, "Cuz, get up here."

"Excuse me," I said to Mom, slowly pushing myself onto my feet. "I think I have to go defend Turk's honor."

As I went up the stairs again, Gregor whisked past me, bowed to Mom, and opened the door.

"Safety to all here," he said. "Please to stay inside tonight. There will be fires."

He slammed out the door.

Turk gave me a look of pure anger as I crept up the ladder.

"He marked me," she said. "Without my permission. He just came up here and said, 'I have been meaning to do this,' reached out his damn claws, and put something on my cheek. Do I have a mark?"

"No," I said. "It's invisible to anybody but a jenti. Anyway, so what? Ileana marked me without my permission. It saved me from being beaten to a bloody pulp by Gregor."

"Yeah, I know all about that," Turk said. "But here's the difference, Cuz, nice and simple so you can understand it: That kind of thing might have worked last winter, but now it doesn't. So why would he do it?"

"Why don't you ask him?" I said.

"I did. I said, 'What the hell was that about?' He said I'd marked him already. Some damn fool thing like that. Then I told him to get out, and he left."

She started pacing back and forth.

"He was just trying to claim me, that's all. Claim me like I'm his property. I'm nobody's thing, damn it.

"He said we'd open the center on Halloween just to show my stuff," Turk went on. "Said he'd go to jail if he had to. I told him I don't need anybody to go to jail for me. Especially him. I do not need anybody."

"Lucky you," I said. "Listen, next time you have to vent, you come to me. I'm not quite up for all this climbing yet."

And I got up and went back to my couch.

That was a quiet night. Inside the house, I mean. Turk didn't come down to dinner, and none of the three of us had much to say.

Outside, though, we heard sirens rushing up and down the streets, and through the windows we saw dull red glares come into the sky, flare up, and die. The smell of smoke came in through the closed doors.

Once, not far off, we heard wolves howling.

"They should impose a curfew," Dad said once.

"Who's going to enforce it?" I said.

If the Mercians and Burgundians were going to fight it out for control of New Sodom, it would take more than the gadje of New Sodom PD to stop them.

But they weren't fighting. Not yet. Not quite. Each side was testing the other, checking out its defenses. Splitting up the town. That's what the fires were about—ash wood for Burgundian fires, oak for Mercian. Fires set on street corners or in the middle of intersections. Then, in the darkness, someone watched to see who came to put them out, and whether new fires were started on top of the ashes of the old.

I couldn't see how the Burgundians could lose. There were about ten of them for every Mercian, and the Burgundians were the jenti who could fly, or turn into wolves. Some could do both. The Mercians turned into selkies. In a stand-up fight, things could only go one way. But was that how the jenti fought their wars?

I went to bed and lay there listening to the sounds of New Sodom slipping into the kind of violence it hadn't seen for centuries.

Over what?

Somebody must know, but there were no answers to be found in that darkness. There was only smoke, and more smoke, making everything darker.

23

I had a crazy dream. I was walking around in New Sodom, and it was now, but it was also then, and it looked like I imagined New Sodom must have looked, with log houses made with overhangs, and muddy streets, and a long rickety bridge leading to Crossfield. So I walked on, and started to smell smoke. I wondered what was burning, but I couldn't see any flames. There was just the smell. I followed it, and came to one of the two-story cabins. The invisible smoke was coming from there. I figured there might be someone inside who needed to be rescued, so I ran to the front door and pushed it open.

Inside were Ileana, Justin, Gregor, Turk, and pretty much everybody else I knew. They were all sitting around a woman in old-fashioned clothes who had to be Mercy Warrener. She was typing away on a laptop, and when I came in, she waved.

"I got your message," she said. "I'm CCing everyone."

I wanted to say, "But don't you smell the fire?" but I couldn't. I just watched Mercy Warrener typing and everyone else smiling at us, while the smell of the smoke got stronger and stronger.

Then there was a rush of heat, the roof started to crack, and I looked up. Flames were spreading across the ceiling, reaching down for us.

"Everybody out!" I shouted.

And I woke up.

I just lay there trembling for a while. Then I reached over and turned on my light.

Morning was starting to come into the sky. I could hear Mom and Dad getting up.

I was too tired to move, but I did it anyway. I was going to go to school today, just to see what was happening. I staggered to the bathroom and ran the shower over me until my heart started beating and my eyes were open. I felt a lot better afterward, and I got dressed and went down to breakfast.

Mom and Dad were sitting closer together than usual. They kept touching each other, and Mom put her hand on my arm every couple of minutes.

"Cody, do you really think you should go to school today?" Dad asked.

"Whatever's going to happen is going to happen," I said. "And I feel sort of okay."

"I'd better check on Turk," Mom said, and went to invade the attic.

She was back in one minute.

"Turk's gone," she said.

Turk had taken her clothes, her sleeping bag, and her car. She'd left a note, and her inflatable *Scream*.

The note was for me.

Hey, Cuz,

This scene is getting too bogus. I'm out of here. Thanks for trying. You were almost human.

Always Leave First,

Turk

PS Say so long to Bat Boy for me.

When I showed it to Mom and Dad, Mom started to cry.

"How could we not have heard her leave?" she said between sobs. "That ladder makes a huge thump when you drop it. And you can hear her car two blocks away. We should have woken up and stopped her."

"I don't think she used the ladder," I said. "I think she went out the window and climbed down the oak in the front yard. And if she was worried about the car waking us up, she could just have pushed it to the end of the street before she started it."

"Anyway, we couldn't have stopped her, short of physical force," Dad said.

"It was physical force that drove her away," Mom said. "Damn them all."

But Mom was wrong. Turk hadn't left because of what had happened to us in Squibnocket, or because of what was going on now. She was too tough for that. She'd left because it looked like the center was going to happen after all. And because Gregor loved her and she loved him. None of that went with her misunderstood artist pose. So she'd driven off, and left me tied up in the tree house again. I wanted to kill her.

"We can't even file a missing persons report for twenty-four hours," Dad was saying. "By that time, she could be a thousand miles from here in any direction. I know a private detective who does good work. He can probably track her down. That way, we can keep tabs on her, at least. I don't know about bringing her back. She's sixteen. There are states where she could declare herself an emancipated minor. It's not like we hold a lot of high cards."

"I'm not sure she should come back," Mom said.

I left the room. Right then, the last thing I wanted was to know where Turk was. I got ready for school, and just before I left the house I stuck Turk's note in my pocket. I was sure to see Gregor, and when I did, I didn't want to spend a lot of time answering questions.

Since I didn't have Turk to take me to school, I waited for the limo. My ride to Vlad was even more luxurious than usual. The car was empty except for me.

When I got to school, the parking lot was almost empty. The campus seemed almost deserted. There seemed to be a knot of people coming and going around the student center, so I went that way.

There was a burned-out oak fire beside the entrance, and an elaborate red, purple, and gold banner flying over the door. The design looked ancient, medieval, maybe. I couldn't tell for sure, but it seemed to be a bloodred dragon outlined in gold.

Inside, Gregor had turned the place into a command post and was running his forces from it. It wasn't just kids standing around talking in small groups and pointing at laptop screens. There were adults there, dangerous-looking Burgundian jenti who seemed to be waiting for orders. And they were all wearing swords. Some of them were carrying crossbows.

Clearly, Mrs. Antonescu's meeting with the Mercians hadn't gone well.

"Duke Gregor is busy," Ilie said as I came in the door.

"My old buddy," I said. "I always knew he'd make good."

"It is his war rank," Ilie said stiffly. "Among us, dukes assume their titles only in times like these."

"Don't you have any grown-ups you could take orders from?" I asked.

"Gregor's father is in Europe," Ilie said. "Gregor is the next in the chain of command."

"Well, congratulations on conquering the student center," I said. "What's your next move, an attack on the library?"

"The duke will secure a base of operations," Ilie said. "Then we will advance as directed. You should go now. You are not one of us."

"Right. When you get a chance, give this to Duke Gregor," I said, handing Ilie the note, and I left.

I went toward the classics building across the empty campus. Vlad had the feel of a Crossfield mill. Something was dying.

"Elliot, wait!" a voice behind me called.

I turned and saw Gregor walking toward me with quick steps. He had the note in his hand.

"What does *bogus* mean in this context?" he said, catching up to me. "I know the word, but it does not seem to fit."

"For God's sake, Gregor," I said. "All it means is that Turk's taken off the way she always does. Her note's an excuse, not an explanation. Deal with it."

"Deal with it? I have nothing to deal with," Gregor said. He crumpled up the note and threw it away. "For the first time, Cody Elliot, I feel sorry for you, having such a person in your family."

"Thanks, Gregor, old pal. That means a lot," I said.

Three jenti suddenly swooped out of a cloud and flew low over our heads. Then they angled away toward Crossfield.

"Gregor," I said, "tell a dumb gadje what's really going on."

"I tell you again, I do not know everything that is going on," Gregor said. "I know only that it is so important to the Mercians that the stupid arts center not open that they are prepared to risk everything in New Sodom to prevent it from doing so. That makes it precious to the Burgundians. To me and my men, at least. So the center will open on Halloween. Then we will see what happens. But I think what happens will be war."

"A war over Turk's junk?" I said. "Anyway, what do you mean, war? You guys are gangs, not armies."

"Jenti do not fight gadje style," Gregor said. "We are quicker and subtler. And very fierce. War is what it is."

"Turk wouldn't like you using her stuff this way," I said.

"Turk is gone," Gregor said. "And the Burgundians did not choose this fight."

I went to my first class and found I was the only person there. Even the teacher was gone, and there was no substitute. It was like that all over Vlad. Of the teachers I knew, only Ms. Vukovitch, Mr. Shadwell, and Mr. Gibbon were at work. They all looked grim, and none of them had much to say to me.

I hung around until the end of the day, then found that the limo service had stopped running. Just stopped. So I had to drag my beaten-up self home, which took a long time.

Which gave me a lot of time to think.

I didn't want to quit. As far as I could see, quitting would only make everything worse. Quitting would be admitting that I was wrong when I wasn't. And even if, after I quit, the jenti stopped giving me the silent treatment, even if Justin and Ileana came to make up, they would still be wrong, and I would still be right, and I would have to act like that wasn't true. But without other people, it was a stupid idea. I wasn't an artist. I didn't need an arts center any more than I needed a cruise ship.

Turk might have been a pain, but at least she'd wanted the center. Now no one did. No one but me, and I'd wanted it for other people. For Mercy Warrener, and Ileana, and, though I hated to admit it, I'd wanted it for Turk.

I kept thinking about Turk's art sitting in the cold dark of the mill, maybe for years, and the wigwam lost there, lost and useless. Unless it went up in flames as part of some jenti battle.

I finally turned the last corner and started up the street to my house. As I climbed up the steps, the door opened and Mom met me.

"Cody, you have company," she said in a loud whisper.

"I do?" I said. If it was Ileana, or even Justin—

"Yes," she said. "And I have no idea who they are."

24

In the living room there were seven kids who looked sort of like jenti but weren't. They were dressed in black and their skin was pale, but they were shorter than jenti, and some of them were wearing sunglasses indoors. Jenti never do that.

They were sprawling on the floor like they hadn't figured out how to use chairs.

One of the girls, who was fat and had her hair roached up into a terrific Mohawk, got up.

"Cody Elliot, we presume?" she said.

"That's me," I said.

"My name is Gelnda," the fat girl said.

"Hi, Glenda," I said. "'S'up?"

"*Gelnda,*" she repeated. "We are the Daughters of the

Crypt Poetry Slam Collective of New Sodom. These ladies are War, Famine, and Death. The tall guy over there is Hieronymus Bosch, and the other one is Basil IX. The one over there under the coffee table is Pestilence."

I saw a pair of long legs sticking out one end of the long brown table by the sofa, and a lot of long, frizzy brown hair coming out from the other end.

"I'm practicing," Pestilence said. "For being in my coffin."

"We are here to be part of your opening," Gelnda went on.

"Whoa," I said. "How did you hear about it?"

"My mother is president of one of the groups you contacted," Famine said. "I heard her talking to another president about it."

"We think it's a valid idea, and we want to be part of it," Basil IX said.

"We will read our stuff," Hieronymus Bosch said.

Pestilence wriggled out from under the table and rolled to her suitcase-sized purse.

"We're serious writers," she said, and held out a thick sheaf of papers.

It was a huge pile of poems, and the way she held it out to me was kind of timid and in-your-face at the same time.

"There are others," Gelnda said. "Musicians. Artists. People like that. We all know each other. We need a place."

"Better than the Screaming Bean," Pestilence said.

"I'm sorry," I said. "We could have used you."

The Daughters looked like I'd just slammed the door in their faces. They were looks of real pain.

Pestilence stuffed the poems back in her purse.

"Yeah, right," she said.

"They always do this to us," Gelnda said. "We're not surprised."

What she said didn't make a lot of sense, but I knew what she was talking about. I'd gone to Cotton Mather High, the gadje school across town, for a semester last year. Guys like these were a joke to the rest of the kids. A mean joke, from what I'd seen. It's dangerous to be different in high school.

"No, really. You sound perfect," I said. "Only there's a slight problem. The jenti are getting ready to kill each other, and from what I hear, their war's going to start at that building. It's going to open on Halloween. But all hell's going to break loose when it does."

"That would explain a lot," Basil IX said.

"The sirens. The fires," Hieronymus Bosch added.

"War," War said. "And I wasn't even invited."

"None of us were," Famine said. "We're just gadje."

"They're going to slaughter each other, and we'll just get stepped on, same as always," Death said.

"Trod on," I said. "As in 'Don't tread on me.'"

Yeah, right. In New Sodom, everybody trod on everybody else. The gadje trod on the jenti, and the Burgundians and the Mercians trod on each other, and now they were both going to use the gadje as pavement for their street fights.

Mercy Warrener got trod on all her life. Goth kids got trod on. For that matter, I had a few footprints on my own face. Sooner or later, everybody was dirt under somebody else's feet. It was probably inevitable.

But accepting it wasn't. You could be a sidewalk, or you could be a rattlesnake. Or at least you could try.

These guys were not what Turk had wanted for the

center. They weren't important, they weren't connected, and they weren't even grown up. But they needed the center and the center needed them.

"Listen," I said. "What if you guys went ahead and showed up? What if we just said, 'Go ahead and start your damn war. We want this place, and we're going to make it happen'?"

"We think that would be cool," Gelnda said.

"Don't say yes so fast," I said. "I have no idea what's going to happen if we do this. The jenti may still start their war. The town may try to do something to stop us. At the very least, we'll be breaking about six laws. But maybe if we show up and do what Mercy—what my cousin and I—wanted to do all along, it may untie this knot New Sodom's tied in."

"Would we be beaten?" Famine asked with a little smile.

"Take a look at me," I said. "And it could get worse."

"Killed for reading poetry," Gelnda said. "Perfect."

"It's no joke," I said. "It could happen."

"It could happen anyway," Pestilence said. "Like you said, nobody knows what's coming next."

"The thing is, we need all those people you talked about," I said. "The more people we have in that mill, the more likely this is to work. We've only got about eight days before Halloween, so we have to start getting the word out now."

"We need a Web site," Pestilence said. "I can do it if you want."

"You've got the job," I said.

"I do good work," Pestilence said.

"You should get started," Gelnda said. "The rest of us will leave now. Everybody go home and start networking."

"Listen, there's one thing I have to ask," I said. "You guys are all Daughters of the Crypt? Even the guys?"

"We took a vote on the name," Gelnda said. "They lost."

"The vote was along gender lines," Hieronymus Bosch said. "It wasn't really fair."

The Daughters of the Crypt, except for Pestilence, took off.

I couldn't believe how calm these kids were. And I didn't think it was because they were clueless about the danger. Maybe there's something about being everybody's in-house loser that helps to make you strong. Anyway, I was glad to have them on my side.

Pestilence and I went up to my room. She sat down at my computer and went straight to work. It was like her brain was hooked up to the screen, and her ideas made a detour through her fingers to get there.

DANGER! ART!

Was the first thing we put up, in dark red letters that emerged one at a time from a field of black. An image of Crossfield before the mills came next, and the words "On a dark and blood-soaked field . . ."

Then an image of the mill.

". . . a new peril to the people of New Sodom has arisen."

Then a picture of one of Turk's art pieces, pulled off the Web.

"It is the threat of art."

We were working so well together it was like we were all one thing—me, Pestilence, the computer, the work we were doing. I felt like I was flying.

And when my mom knocked on the door and asked if my friend was staying for dinner, I automatically said, "Sure."

Then I said, "Can you?"

And Pestilence said, "Thanks, yeah. I think I should. We still have to do your podcast."

I was sure Mom and Dad would figure Pestilence was a little weird. After all, she was a little weird. But there was only one truly weird thing that night: Pestilence and Mom hit it off right away.

"I want to hear all about your poetry," Mom said. "I wrote a lot when I was in college."

My mother wrote poetry? How come she never told me?

"Why did you stop?" Pestilence wanted to know.

"My inspiration was Sylvia Plath. Like a lot of young women then. I'm afraid I wasn't very original. And when I got married and had Cody—my life just seemed so pleasant, I felt like a fraud writing all that dark stuff."

"Sylvia Plath had a husband and children," Pestilence said. "She stayed dark. Very dark."

"That's true," Mom said, and leaned forward with her chin on her hand. "Who inspires you?"

"I feel, like, a spiritual affinity for the Anglo-Saxon poets," Pestilence said. "But I wouldn't say they inspire me. It's just that they understood fate."

Dad turned his wineglass in his hand and said, "Give us something."

Pestilence stood up and shouted:

Still life.
That's what they call it.
Slice of life.
An old Dutch painting.
Tulips dead four hundred years.
A vase that broke when a bomb blew up the museum
*   it was in*

Back in World War II.
And crawling across the rotted table a bug that didn't
    live through winter.
Slice of life?
Slice of death.

"Not bad," Dad said.

"I can see why you like the Anglo-Saxons," Mom said.

"It's like having our own gleeman," Dad said. "Or glee-woman, I guess."

"What's a gleeman?" I said.

"A poet hired to entertain the dinner guests in an Anglo-Saxon mead hall," Dad said.

I looked at Dad in surprise. I wasn't used to him knowing things except law stuff.

"I married *her*." Dad shrugged and cocked his head toward Mom. "It's been educational."

"Just a minute, please." Mom smiled and ducked her head. "I'll be right back."

She got up and almost ran up the stairs.

"Have you read the Burton Raffel translation of *Beowulf*?" Pestilence asked Dad. "He was also a lawyer, I think, before he switched to poetry."

Pestilence and Dad launched into this whole thing about *Beowulf,* and whether the dragon is Beowulf's own unacknowledged fear and whether the Anglo-Saxon warriors are the modern intellect, and a whole lot of other stuff I must have been absent for the day they taught it in school.

"Those Saxons are just like lawyers," Dad said, sounding excited. "Greedy, conscienceless, out for loot. Beowulf and Elliot, attorneys at law."

"You probably know the word *attorney* is literally 'at

torney'—at tournament," Pestilence said. "It goes back to the times when you hired a mercenary to fight for you in trial by combat."

"Hasn't changed," Dad said. "When I go into the courtroom—"

They stopped when Mom walked in.

She was carrying some worn black notebooks, and she had a shy smile on her face.

"Some of my old things," she said.

"Read us something," Pestilence said.

Mom flipped open one of the notebooks and said, "Oh, this is really bad. But I was so proud of it when I wrote it."

The lonely trees are still and stark.
The death-cloak snow lies on the ground.
The pallid sun goes down to dark
And silence is the only sound.
My heart has wandered from this home
And found no better sky or earth,
So I return to it alone,
Contented with my share of dearth.

" 'Death-cloak snow,' " Pestilence said. "I wish I'd thought of that."

I wished I'd never heard it. It was embarrassing, like walking in on Mom and Dad kissing. I was hoping we'd change the subject, but Mom and Pestilence were on a roll. First Pestilence recited a poem, then Mom did one of hers. Then they'd say something like "That broken window is a good image," or "I really like the assonance in that last line."

They went on like that for an hour, with Dad paying

attention to every word, and me hoping they'd run out of them.

But when it was over, I'd never seen my mom so happy. No, that wasn't it. I'd never seen her happy in the way she was happy then. And it was beautiful. And Pestilence looked just the same way.

They might have gone on like that all night, but Pestilence said, "You know, Cody, we ought to get back to work on that project," and stood up.

"Right," I said. "Homework."

"Homework?" Dad said. "How can you two have homework together? I thought Pestilence went to Cotton Mather."

"That's right," Pestilence said. "Cody studied something last year that we're only getting to this year in one of my AP classes. He's helping me with it."

Pestilence was smooth, very smooth.

Anyway, we did the podcast, with Pestilence being the interviewer, and asking me everything about the center. I thought it was pretty dull, actually, but when we played it back, I sounded like I really knew what I was talking about. It was awesome.

"It still needs some more work," Pestilence said. "But I can do a lot of it at home. We'll be up by day after tomorrow at the latest. Then we'll see who responds."

"Pestilence," I said, "this was great. It would have taken me a week to do this, and parts of it I couldn't have done at all. Thanks."

"This has been a really good night for me," Pestilence said. "I hardly ever—well, never—get this kind of interest at home."

But that wasn't the end of the evening. Not quite. Mom

caught Pestilence on her way out the door and invited her to come back and bring her poetry and her friends.

"Do you mean for a slam?" Pestilence asked.

"Maybe a slam, maybe a salon. We'll see how it goes," Mom said. "I've never been to a slam."

"I've never been to a salon," Pestilence said. "But, whatever it is, I'll pass your invitation along. Anyway, Cody and I will be seeing more of each other."

Oh, good. More chances to be embarrassed. But I needed her. More than that, I liked her.

"Right," I said. "Pestilence needs lots of help."

"Let me give you a ride home," Dad said. "It's not a good night to be out alone."

But Pestilence turned him down.

"I don't live that far," she said. "And the night's got my back."

I walked her to the door, and out onto the porch. It was cold, and the wind blew Pestilence's hair across her face.

"Hey, your old guys are really cool," she said.

"They are?" I said. I mean, I loved my parents. They were my parents. But they were not cool.

"Your mom is like this dark lake of poetry and words," she said. "And it goes real deep. And your dad—he's a dragon-killer."

"My dad?" A nuisance, often. Funny, frequently. A get-down lawyer, sure. But a dragon-killer?

"Sure," Pestilence said. "You saw how excited he got talking about *Beowulf*. He put down his wineglass and put his hand on his belt."

"So?" I said.

"So he was reaching for his sword," Pestilence said.

"He thinks he's in lawyering for the gold, but that's not it, really. He likes going up against something bigger than he is and killing it. Then he takes the gold to show that he did it."

Pestilence looked me up and down.

"And then there's you," she said. "I haven't got you figured out yet."

The way she looked at me made me kind of nervous.

"Maybe there isn't that much to figure out," I said.

"Yeah," Pestilence said. "That's what I'd say, except there's this whole thing with the center. I think you might be kind of an ignorant Diaghilev."

"Okay, I am ignorant," I said. "What's a dog leaf?"

"Diaghilev was the impresario who established the Ballets Russes back—I don't know, about 1905, I think," Pestilence said. "He hired Stravinsky to write music, Bakst to do sets and costumes, then he got the greatest dancers in the world to work for him. They turned ballet into something it had never been before. He couldn't dance, he couldn't compose, he couldn't even sew. But he made it all happen. Ballets Russes, man. You should know about that. Diaghilev and Nijinsky."

"What? Who's Nijinsky?" I said, scoring another point on the ignorance meter.

"Vaslav Nijinsky. Diaghilev's greatest dancer. Greatest male dancer ever. They were lovers."

"Oh," I said. "Well, I guess I'm not that much of a Diaghilev. No lover named Vaslav."

"No," Pestilence said.

Then all of a sudden she was wrapping her arms around me and giving me a long kiss.

I kissed her back, and it was like holding a snake in my arms. A very warm and friendly snake.

"G'night," she said, and sort of skipped down the steps and out to the sidewalk.

I stood there tingling and confused, listening to her steps fade.

Finally, I got ready for bed.

Lying there, I realized something. Tonight was the first night I'd been happy in a long time. All of a sudden, I wasn't carrying the center all by myself. And there was that kiss. Oh, yeah. There was that kiss. I didn't know what to make of it yet, but I was still tingling from it, almost half an hour later.

And there was something else that had come out of tonight. The look on my mother's face. Dad's good talk. It hadn't mattered that Pestilence was a stranger, and even stranger than most. Art, poetry, had cut right through everything to make us all friends and make us happy to be together.

And if Mom and Dad could get into a night with Pestilence, who knew what real people might do?

"Hey, Mercy," I said to the night. "We're gonna do it. Don't be late."

25

I didn't see Pestilence again that week. She e-mailed me a lot, and sent me updates to the Web site every day, but there was no mention of kissing at all. She was strictly business online.

Meanwhile, Dad got word on Turk. She was in Manhattan overnight, then in Brooklyn, then in New Jersey. Then the detective lost track of her for a day, and when he located her again, she was in Baltimore.

"She's not doing anything," Dad said. "She just checks into a motel, gets some gas, and drives on. Maybe she's heading for Mexico to get some more tattoos."

Then we lost her again, and this time the detective couldn't find her. Mom and Dad were worried, but I wasn't. Not much. I figured the detective had tipped his hand somehow and Turk had thrown him off her trail. Wherever she was, she was probably enjoying the feeling of being followed.

As for me, I was wondering if Diaghilev had ever had to beat people off with a stick.

Once the Web site was up and linked to, a lot of kids started to find out about the center. We were getting comments from people in Connecticut and Rhode Island as well as from the towns around New Sodom. Poets and painters and performance artists and dancers were checking in and signing on. The warnings about what might happen on Halloween didn't scare them off. Some of them sounded like they were hoping for the worst.

I made up charts of every floor to figure out who could perform where. They filled in fast.

I told Gregor at school the next day. He was okay with the whole thing, which surprised me.

"Excellent idea," he said when I told him. "The artists will meet under the wings of the Burgundians that night. The Mercians will be shamed and stay away, or they will come and we will defend the gadje artists against them. Either way, it will be our first victory. Thank you."

"Man," I said. "I am just trying to get the center open."

"I know," Gregor said. "But sometimes, Cody Elliot, you accomplish more with your stupid ideas than the cleverest jenti. This will be one of those times."

"Just one thing," I said. "Let me cut the police tape. If the police show up, they might not want to arrest everybody. Maybe they'll just take the one who let the rest in. I don't want any confusion about who that was."

"As you like," Gregor said. "I think the police will be the least of our concerns. If they are wise, they will not come to Crossfield that night. There are very few jenti among them, and if we decline to be arrested, there will be not much they can do."

Another pleasant possibility for opening night.

I went over to the classics building. My feet made the only sound in the hall. Vlad didn't feel like a school anymore. All the paintings on the walls and the expensive architecture seemed to belong to some other time all of a sudden.

As I passed Mr. Shadwell's room, he came to the door.

"Ah, Elliot. I was hoping to see you. Please come in," he said.

"I have to get to class," I said.

"I don't believe you have a first period this morning," Mr. Shadwell said. "No one from the math department is here. And I have something to discuss with you. Please."

I went in. Some of the chairs had been pulled out from behind the desks and arranged in a circle by the blackboard.

Mr. Shadwell pulled out his cell and dialed. "He's here. Come right over."

"Uh-oh," I thought. "The gadje's in trouble again."

I expected to see cops, or maybe sword-waving jenti, come through the door. But the only thing that happened was that Ms. Vukovitch and Mrs. Warrener appeared about a minute later and smiled at me.

We sat down, with Mr. Shadwell across from me and the others on my right and left.

At least I wasn't going to get beaten, arrested, or stabbed.

Mr. Shadwell leaned forward and said, almost in a whisper, "Tell me, Elliot. Is it true that you are planning poetry readings at that mill of yours?"

Huh?

"We have a slam set up," I said. "Some kids from Cotton Mather are going to read."

Shadwell took a deep breath.

"As you may recall, I write epics," he said. "I wish to offer myself as a part of the evening's events. If you still have room."

"Wow," I said. "Are you serious?"

"I do not speak lightly of my poetry, Elliot," he said.

"No, of course you don't," I said, remembering last year, when he'd read us long chunks of the poem he was working on. "I mean, sure, you're in. But you know—it could get ugly."

"Precisely, Elliot," Mr. Shadwell said. "That is why we wish to be there."

"All three of you?" I said. "But it's dangerous."

"Not all jenti approve of this"—and he used a jenti word I didn't know but that sounded terrible—"that is going on in New Sodom. This Mercian-Burgundian rubbish. We wish to demonstrate our opposition to it. We—"

"It's like this, gadje boy—excuse me—Master Cody," Ms. Vukovitch said. "Some of us think your center is a real cool idea. We want to be there."

"Burgundians and Mercians together, Cody," Mrs. Warrener finished. "Doing things for the love of doing them."

"Okay," I said. "But what do you want to do?"

"As you know, Mrs. Warrener is an accomplished pianist," Mr. Shadwell said. "She will accompany Ms. Vukovitch, who will sing that night. And she has something of her own to offer as well. An original composition."

"Ms. Vukovitch is a singer?" I said.

"In my youth, when I was still beautiful," Ms. Vukovitch

purred, "I sang in cafés all over Europe. They used to say I made the piano smoke."

"We don't have a piano," I said.

"Elliot, you've lived here long enough to know that things like pianos turn up where they're needed," Mr. Shadwell said with a little grin.

"You mean like Dumpsters?" I asked.

"No idea what you mean," he said.

I couldn't tell whether he was lying or not.

"But in any case, thank you, Elliot," he said. "I look forward to Halloween this year. Very much, in fact."

They didn't look like heroes. Mr. Shadwell was short for a Burgundian, and bald, and maybe just a little pompous. Ms. Vukovitch looked like the hero's girlfriend, if he was a very lucky hero. And Mrs. Warrener was as delicate as an autumn leaf. But they were heroes. I had no idea what this was costing them among the jenti, but the price had to be high.

"Thank you all," I said. "See you on Halloween."

I went into an empty room, took out my charts, and looked to see where I could put Mrs. Warrener and Mr. Shadwell. The piano would have to go on the ground floor somewhere, so I moved the Sixty-Minute Shakespeare Theater Company from the north wing to the third floor, next to Gregor's place. I already had two art exhibits slotted in for the walls, but people would just have to share the space. Mr. Shadwell I put in the same second-floor space as the Daughters, and gave them alternate quarter-hours all night long. I hoped that would work.

Before I put my charts away, I looked at them again, checking everything. I had drawn them on graph paper, and had made neat, precise notes of times, places, groups, and artists. It all looked so organized. But there was more going on than I knew about, maybe more than anyone knew about.

This Halloween was going to be long on trick.

26

Halloween came. I was jumpy as a cat all day. I couldn't concentrate. Or actually, I was concentrating on the coming night, and on what could go wrong, which was everything. I wondered if this was how Diaghilev had felt.

Finally, I decided to go over to the mill and worry there. And, because it was Halloween, I took Turk's inflatable *Scream* along with me. My date for the evening.

Getting to Crossfield without Turk's car was a pain. The buses had stopped running across the river a few days before. I had to take one that stopped five blocks from the river and turned back. And it was slow, slow, slow. The streets outside the windows were empty. In another year, there would have been people in costumes—witches, ghosts, aliens, everything but vampires. Not this year.

When I walked up to the bridge, there were two Burgundians guarding it. Guys I knew slightly from Vlad. They were wearing armbands and swords. Each one had a massive crossbow on his shoulder.

Where had they gotten that stuff from? Were there secret arsenals around New Sodom? And why such ancient weapons? And what weapons would the Mercians use?

"I'm here on business," I said.

"Pass, gadje," one of the guards said. "Duke Gregor told us to permit it."

Around the mill there were six more guards, and four on the roof. But the yellow police tape was uncut.

Vladimir was there.

"It begins," he said, and handed me a knife. "This is Duke Gregor's blade. He asks that you use it for this work."

"Here goes," I said, and cut the tape. It fluttered to the ground and danced there in the wind.

I unlocked the door of the mill and went in.

Cold, stale air blew in my face. The frame of the wigwam looked exactly like the skeleton of some weird beast in the fading light. Except for it, and for Turk's stuff hanging on the walls, the place was barren. It felt lonely and lost. For a second I wished Turk was back, complaining and giving orders no one listened to.

I set *The Scream* inside the wigwam. Then I went downstairs and turned on the turbines, then the master switches. Lights came on overhead. The building was coming to life.

I went back upstairs and met a crew of jenti with brooms and mops. Ilie was in charge of them.

"Duke Gregor has sent us," he said. "You wish us to begin now?"

They whipped through the place while I went around turning on the rest of the lights. As soon as they were done with the first floor, a big truck pulled up out front and a couple of gadje got out.

"Where do you want us to put the piano, kid?" one of them asked.

There was even a candelabrum to put on top of it.

When Mrs. Warrener showed up, she ran her fingers over the keys, nodded, and started to play. Something sad and full of moonlight.

Ilie and his guys put down their brooms and came over to listen. We were still listening when Gregor showed up.

He was wearing combat fatigues and carrying a sword.

Mrs. Warrener beckoned him over. Quietly, he unbuckled his sword belt and joined us.

Mrs. Warrener started playing one of those mysterious songs in high jenti, and Gregor sang. Ilie lit the candles and turned off the lights in the room. Then the other jenti joined in, singing the chorus and making the walls shake. It was beautiful and sad, and when Gregor hit a high note that was just south of a wail, I shivered.

Gregor bowed, his guys bowed to him, and they left as quietly as they'd come.

"We indulge ourselves," Gregor said. "Tonight, with everyone here and electric lights, it will not be the same."

"It will be great," I said.

Mrs. Warrener smiled.

"Oh, Cody," she said. "I so hope nothing bad happens tonight."

"In any case, we shall finish a few songs at least before— before whatever must happen happens," Gregor said.

Mrs. Warrener blew out the candles.

The three of us stood in the near dark, not talking or moving. It was like we were waiting for something to end and something to begin, and it wouldn't be right to rush it.

"*Un ange passe,*" Mrs. Warrener said.

"What?" I said.

"An angel passes," Mrs. Warrener explained. "It's what the French say about a moment like that."

"We could use a few angels tonight," I said.

"In any case," Gregor said, "it is time to see who we do get."

When we turned the lights back on, I saw how much Ilie's cleaning crew had done. The redbrick walls shone and the windows glittered. Even the old dark wood of the floors glowed. Turk's art seemed to leap off the walls. The old building was ready to party. And what would happen tonight was about to start.

There was a timid knock on the open door.

Justin stood there with a package under his arm.

"Hi, Mom. Hi, Cody," he said.

"'S'up?" I said.

"Who let you past, Mercian?" Gregor said.

"I'm not a Mercian," Justin said. "I told 'em, whatever they were planning, I wasn't part of it anymore."

"Oh, thank God," Mrs. Warrener said.

"Cody, I'm sorry," Justin said. "I know that's pretty inadequate, but I am. If you don't want me here, just say so. But I had to come and tell you and Mom."

"Well . . . I guess it's a big deal to be a Mercian," I said.

"I thought it was," Justin said. "Maybe three hundred years ago it meant something good."

"You didn't know," Mrs. Warrener said. "And you thought they were something else. And when I tried to tell you, you didn't want to hear."

"I guess not," Justin said.

Mrs. Warrener held out her arms and Justin walked into them.

"I know it's hard without your father," she said. "I know what you were hoping to find."

Gregor and I looked away. This kind of thing didn't usually happen with old-time New Englanders. But right now, the two of them didn't care who saw them.

And maybe another angel passed just then.

Justin took something out of his pocket and handed it to Gregor.

"Take it if you want it," he said. "I'm through with it."

It was a silver eagle with two heads.

"I do not want this trash," Gregor said. But he didn't seem to know what to do with it.

"Not my problem," Justin said.

"Here, gadje. Take this. Please," Gregor said. "Get it out of my hand. A souvenir of something. Of your opening."

I took it and put it in my pocket. A souvenir of getting a friend back.

"Well, if you stick around here, I'm going to put you to work," I said. "Bandaged hand or not."

"In that case, here," Justin said, and handed me the package. "Thought you might like to have it for tonight."

It was a tube of brown paper tied up with white string that looked like it had been knotted a long time ago. I cut the string and started to unwrap whatever it was.

"Careful," Justin said. "It's kind of old."

Mrs. Warrener gasped.

A bolt of cloth started to appear, and Justin came forward to help me unroll it.

When we were done, we were each holding one end of an old flag. The field was red, and in black letters at the top it said, NEW SODOM. At the bottom it said, DON'T TREAD ON ME. In between were two rattlesnakes twined together around an angel.

"Mercy Warrener's flag," Justin said. "Mom gave it to me about a year ago, said I could do what I liked with it. Been thinking about it. I thought maybe we could fly it here."

"We have to," I said. "Can't open this place without Mercy."

"The flag expresses an excellent sentiment," Gregor said. "Fly it."

We refolded the flag and went up to the third floor, with Gregor and Mrs. Warrener. We opened the window next to the flagpole, and ran the flag out. It streamed sideways in the wind and the dusk.

I saw a couple of vans pull up out front.

"There are the artists," Gregor said. "You had better go and tell them where to set up."

As I went downstairs, Justin was beside me.

"Cody, I'm pretty sure something bad's going to happen tonight," he began.

"I know," I said. "We'll deal."

"Right," Justin said.

And just like that, everything was the way it had been.

By now there were six trucks and vans in front of the center, and paintings and sculptures and video equipment were exploding out of them. I put Justin in charge of the second floor and Gregor on the third, to make sure everybody set up in the right places. I took the first floor myself.

Mrs. Warrener greeted every arrival and directed them to parking.

So far, so good.

Meanwhile, the Burgundians were thickening outside, surrounding the building, flying overhead. It was sinister.

But inside, the old mill was filled with sounds of hammering and loud voices. Happy, excited voices. In less than an hour, half the walls were covered, and the floors were filling up. More vans came, and by dark the old mill looked like a gallery. The piano was surrounded by wild and crazy stuff, and folding chairs were being set up in the empty spaces.

Folding chairs? I hadn't ordered any folding chairs. But they were coming off a big truck that said NEW SODOM PARTY AND BANQUET SUPPLIES, and Mrs. Warrener was seeing to it that they got put where they were wanted.

"Hey," I asked one of the guys setting up, "who paid for all this?"

"Don't ask me, man, I just truck the stuff out and set the stuff up, y'know?" he said.

Then the poets and actors and musicians started to arrive and I didn't have time to think about chairs.

The Shakespeareans went on the third floor. The Daughters' slam was supposed to be on the second. Pestilence gave a slow wink and squeezed my arm as she went by. A rock group called Styx of One didn't even have a reservation. I found them a place in the basement. They didn't seem to mind.

Mr. Shadwell showed up wearing a tuxedo. Ms. Shadwell was with him, hanging on his arm and smiling like her inner wolf.

"Where do you want me, Elliot?" Mr. Shadwell roared,

and I sent him up to where the Daughters were already hollering their poems to an empty room.

I could hear the soft throb of the rock band coming up through the floor, and the chat of voices all around me as the artists checked out each other's work. Once in a while, a few loud words came down from the gallery where the poets were. The evening felt like it wanted to take off and fly. It was trying its wings, seeing if it could get airborne on this dark, windy night.

A few visitors drifted in. Some of them were parents or friends, but a few were gadje who'd heard about tonight and wanted to check it out. They came in with their shoulders hunched, looking around like they were scouting for booby traps.

Then Ms. Vukovitch arrived in a black dress that could have slithered across the floor by itself if she hadn't been in it. She gave me a smile and sauntered down the rows of Turk's paintings.

"Hey, Ms. Vukovitch," I said, catching up to her. "Would you like a job?"

"Does it pay better than teaching science?" she asked.

"It doesn't pay at all," I said. "I need someone to greet these gadje as they come in. Make them feel less nervous."

"Sure." Ms. Vukovitch shrugged. "Anything for the arts, gadje boy," and she intercepted the next couple who walked in. After she'd done that a few times, a lot of the men were smiling. Most of the women weren't. They kept looking at Ms. Vukovitch and frowning. But at least they weren't worrying about their safety.

Almost six-forty-five. In another half hour, Mrs. Warrener and Ms. Vukovitch would start their part of the evening, if it lasted that long. Anyway, things seemed to be going along okay down here. I thought I'd better check out the second floor.

There was a modern-dance concert going on at one end. Seven or eight kids moving around to some canned music. No audience, at least not yet. I gave them a thumbs-up and moved on to the poetry slam.

Now, here there was an audience. Mr. Shadwell, Ms. Shadwell, and four people who looked like they were parents of some of the Daughters. Basil IX was open and pumping:

"Where do they go,
The old TV shows?
They go on forever
Getting weaker and weaker
Out across space,
Falling apart, losing the meaning
They never had
Till they fall off the edge
Of the universe.
No need to rehearse
All those old shows.
They make just as much sense
When they fall off the edge
As the babble of dying stars."

There was a lot more like that.

Everyone clapped, then Basil IX sat down and Mr. Shadwell got up.

"I would like to begin with a few lines from my first epic, *Penobscot,*" he said. "This passage describes the coming to

Vinland of Leif Ericsson in 1003, more or less. It was my first, not completely successful attempt to merge the elements of Anglo-Saxon prosody, which I greatly admire, with the stylistic elements of Walt Whitman's verse."

He took a deep breath and began.

"The shore-stones wave-ravaged, the land unnamed.
No, not unnamed, but known by name
Never to be known by men who came
In swift sea-skimmers sent from far fjord
In hopeful reconnoiter for a richer steading.
Their name they gave it: Vinland! Vinland the good.
And where they found safe harbor as seemed fair
To men salt-crusted from long days upon
The gray and friendless whale-road, they dragged
Their dragon ship ashore. Its keel-mark on sand
The first stroke of the first rune of their first kenning."

The Daughters started doing little things in pantomime behind Mr. Shadwell's back after about the first two minutes. Gelnda put her head between her knees. Hieronymus Bosch put his finger down his throat. Death and Famine hugged each other and cried. Basil IX tried to gouge out his eyes.

Some of the audience shook their heads, trying to get their kids to stop. Some smiled. A couple laughed. Finally, most of them got up and wandered away. Mr. Shadwell plowed on until his time was up. Then he bowed a little bow and sat down, and his wife clapped.

Gelnda got up and raised her fists over her head and shrieked. It was a good shriek, but apparently not what she was after. Because she did it again, long and wavering like a siren. Then she shrieked three more times, each time on a higher note. Then she screamed in short little bursts like a machine gun. She kept making up new screams until her voice started to give out on her. Then, in a rasp that we could barely hear, she said,

"The earth is our mother.
Let's make her scream."

And she sat down.

All the Daughters clapped, and both remaining pairs of moms and dads. Mr. Shadwell sat leaning forward with his hand on his chin and a frown on his face.

Hieronymus Bosch got up next, and ran through something about garbage. That was the whole poem, a list of what was in his garbage can. At the end of it, he said, "With thanks to Walt Whitman," and bowed to Mr. Shadwell.

Mr. Shadwell sat back and crossed his arms.

I wasn't sure I liked the way this was going. I didn't want to see Mr. Shadwell get dissed. Or trod on. But then Justin put his hand on my arm and whispered, "Just thought you ought to know. Your cousin's here."

27

If Turk was back, I'd better know why. Mr. Shadwell would just have to be on his own for a while.

"Thanks," I said. "Come on."

We went downstairs.

Turk had come in with a new wave of visitors. Most of them were jenti, and all of those were Burgundians. Half of them had their patented jenti sneers firmly in place. The other half looked like they didn't know what they thought.

"Thanks for coming," I said to as many as I could reach while I searched for Turk. "Poetry and theater upstairs. If you hang around here for a few more minutes, we'll have some traditional jenti stuff. Thanks, thanks."

Turk was lounging around in her art exhibit with her hands in her pockets. She looked exactly the same, which surprised me for some reason. Maybe because it felt like she'd been gone for a long time.

When she saw me, she smiled and waved.

"Hi, Cuz," she said. "Not bad so far."

"Do Mom and Dad know you're back?" I asked.

"I'm not back," she said. "I just came to our opening. I'll take off again when it's over."

"We'll talk about that," I said. "You left me holding the bag on this thing. You owe me."

"It was good for you," Turk laughed. "Forced you to act on your own. If you'd had me here to do it all for you, you wouldn't have learned anything."

I said something in jenti that would have made her slug me if she'd known what it meant.

"By the way, where's the big guy?" Turk said. "You know, the dumb one?"

"He's around," I said. "Patrolling. Checking up. Being a duke. By the way, a war's supposed to start tonight."

"Cool," Turk said. "That ought to get us noticed."

From the other side of the room, Ms. Vukovitch's throaty voice was filling the air with sexy-sounding songs.

Turk and I went over that way.

Most of the chairs were filled. Jenti and gadje were sitting close together, leaning forward, caught in the music.

Ms. Vukovitch finished her song and smiled.

"Thank you for coming tonight," she said. "We all know this is not a usual night. Halloween never is. And this is not a usual Halloween. No one knows what's going to happen. But then, do we ever really know? This is a song about not knowing, and finding out that you do not know. I used to sing it in Vienna about a hundred years ago."

While she was singing, Gregor came in to the room.

When he saw Turk, he stopped moving. He looked like he had when Justin handed him the Mercian eagle. He didn't know what to do.

As Ms. Vukovitch finished her next song, he went over to Mrs. Warrener and whispered to her and Ms. Vukovitch.

"We have a request from our young duke," Ms. Vukovitch announced. "A traditional jenti lament. It is the story of a jenti's betrayal by an untrustworthy gadje. It is a song we all know well."

Now Gregor looked straight at Turk, and she stared right back at him. They were eyeing each other like a couple of snakes.

The audience kept growing. People were filtering in from outside and being drawn to the music. There had been thirty; now there were more than twice that.

There was nothing to do here.

I went back upstairs to see what was happening at the poetry thing.

Mr. Shadwell was just getting up.

"This is a very special evening for all of us," he said to the near-empty seats. "Something new is beginning here. One can feel it. And the voice of that thing is in the throats of these young poets. We can hear it calling to us. I, for one, intend to answer that call."

And he changed into a wolf.

And he stood there, a wolf in a tuxedo.

"Xhat is better," he announced, leaning his forelegs on the podium. His voice was thick now, and very deep. He couldn't form words the same way with his long jaws, but it didn't seem to matter. He had everyone's attention now, even the Daughters'. Especially the Daughters'.

"Now I should like to recite from memory a fine

Amerhican poem by Allen Ginsberg. Which some of you may recognize. I refer to his masterwork, *Howl*."

Howl. I'd heard of it, but I'd never read it. Now I heard the whole thing, page after page of it, coming out of the jaws of a thick, gray wolf with fierce green eyes. Allen Ginsberg, whoever he was, couldn't have asked for a better voice for his words, even if Mr. Shadwell couldn't pronounce them all in the usual way.

A few people drifted in to see what the noise was. None of them left. There is nothing like a wolf reciting poetry to hold a crowd.

When Mr. Shadwell got to the end of the poem, and finished on a high, wailing note that sounded like it was aimed at the moon, nobody clapped. Nobody did anything.

Then Pestilence screamed, "Far out, old man!" and ran over and hugged him.

Gelnda jumped up and down. Basil IX thumped Mr. Shadwell on the back. So did Hieronymus Bosch. Famine, Death, and War clapped. So did everyone else. All five of them. But it didn't matter how few there were. They were loving the moment.

And at the door, clapping and cheering, was my mom.

"Mom, what are you doing here?" I said when I got over to her.

"Having the best time I've had since we came to New Sodom," she said. "Cody, we had no idea."

"Where's Dad?" I said.

"Down at the concert listening to Ms. Vukovitch," Mom said.

"Mom, I'd really like you to go," I said. "It could get dangerous tonight."

"We'll leave if you do," Mom said.

"I can't. I'm sort of in charge," I said.

"Then stop trying to tell me what to do, Cody," Mom said.

But now the Daughters were standing in a knot around Mr. Shadwell, and he was waving his hands around saying, "Xhe work of xhese young people, crude as it is at first glance, contains many of xhe elemental strengxhs of poetry. Exactly xhe elements I try to inculcate in my students. We have heard vivid, promising xhings here tonight. And we have heard xhem because one young man, a forhmer student of mine"—he nodded at me—"will not be intimidated or defeated. It has been said that poetry is an act of courage in a dark world. Well, an act of courage in a dark world is a poem. And we must all salute—"

Everyone was looking at me.

"Mr. Shadwell, do something else," I shouted.

"Right," Gelnda rasped. "Do something else."

"It's your turn," Mr. Shadwell told her. "But if you like, we can alternate. I xhink I went on too long with *Penobscot*. Let's do shorter xhings and see if we can maintain xhis energy level."

"Everybody: one page or less," Gelnda said. "Pestilence, you're up."

The poets started to bounce their lines back and forth in short bursts. And whatever one of the Daughters said, Mr. Shadwell had something from an epic to come back with. It might not have made any sense, but it didn't matter. Wave-ravaged shore-stones and rants about global warming *sounded* right together. Something was happening that didn't have anything to do with slamming or reciting. People were loving the play between the kids and the old gray wolf. They made so much noise applauding that more people came to see what was going on. The place was filling up.

"Gotta go, Mom," I said. "By the way, Turk's downstairs."

"Where is she? Is she all right?" Mom said.

"As good as she ever is," I said.

Mom put her hand to her face and breathed deeply. Her shoulders dropped, and when she took her hand away, her face was almost happy.

"I suppose we should have expected it," she said. "That girl is never going to miss a chance to show off. But thank God she's back."

"She's over by her paintings, if you want to spank her," I said.

"Thanks," Mom said. "Maybe I will."

I checked out the Sixty-Minute Shakespeare company. Every Shakespeare play was getting done in two minutes. The modern dancers were taking a break and watching the actors run through their show for the second time. People from downstairs were wandering in and laughing. Okay, nothing to take care of here. I went downstairs.

Ms. Vukovitch was finishing her last song. Maybe a hundred people were there to hear it. Turk wasn't one of them. I saw her across the way, looking at someone else's sculpture, a sort of cascade of broken glass and copper wire.

Gregor was gone. Probably he was outside again.

The applause started slow, jenti style, with everyone clapping together. Then it got faster and faster until it turned into a wave. A wave that went on for five minutes. I timed it.

Then Ms. Vukovitch announced, "This concludes the

first part of the program. The next is a new piano composition, 'Fantasia on Three Folk Themes,' by Julia Warrener."

Justin went over to turn pages for his mom.

She began to play, and it sounded like the same music Gregor had sung before the evening began—without the words, of course. But she took the music and wove it into something else, playing it faster and faster. She was turning the sad songs into music for dancing.

And then, a couple of the jenti did just that.

I'd seen jenti dance once before, at Ileana's birthday party last year. It had been amazing. They'd turned from these quiet, cool people with about as much life as department store window dummies into hawks, spinning across the dance floor and throwing each other at the sky.

That's what happened now. One couple, then another, then a whole line of couples swinging around the gallery.

Somehow, the chairs disappeared. Mrs. Warrener's music crashed louder and louder as the jenti feet thumped on the old wooden planks.

Then Ms. Vukovitch took my dad's hand. And he danced. He didn't dance like a jenti, but he danced, and Ms. Vukovitch didn't pick him up and throw him over her head or anything like that, but everyone was watching the jenti and the gadje dancing together. And that did it. In another minute, everybody but me, Turk, and Gregor and his guys was out on the floor.

The dancers who'd been watching the actors came downstairs to see what was going on and jumped in. One girl grabbed Gregor's hand. The next time I saw her, she was being flung between him and Vladimir in time to the music, soaring up like a beautiful bird.

Then the singer of Styx of One came up, looking like he couldn't believe what was happening.

He grabbed my arm.

"Hey, man, I came up to complain about the noise," he said.

"What noise?" I said. "Deal with it."

He looked around at the swirl of bodies and shook his head.

"All right, man, we will," he said.

In a few minutes the band was back, with their drums and their amps, and they started playing along with Mrs. Warrener.

Now everybody in the rest of the building was pouring in. The poets came down, and Pestilence grabbed me, and we started dancing. I saw Mr. and Ms. Shadwell close by. She'd changed into a wolf, too, and they were jumping and chasing each other around so fast it was like two streaks of red and gray flowing together. The actors came in next, and they started doing a kind of Elizabethan partner dance, but sped up to match the music, and pretty soon they had jenti learning it.

After a very long time that was too short, the first jenti-gadje band in the history of New Sodom crashed to a stop. Everybody cheered. We cheered ourselves and the band and each other. Gadje hugged jenti, and jenti smiled. A lot of fangs were out, but nobody seemed to mind. It was excitement, not hunger.

Mrs. Warrener and the band's singer had their heads together. After a minute, she announced, "The group and I have decided upon a set. Please stay and rock out if you like."

And the music started again.

"This is quite a night, Diaghilev," Pestilence said.

"Yeah," I said. "Maybe that angel who was passing by decided to stay."

"Huh?" Pestilence said.

I explained about *un ange passe*.

"That's my last name," Pestilence said. "DiAngelo."

"Oh," I said. "What's your first name?"

"Angela," Pestilence said. "But never call me that. Not if you want to live."

Angela DiAngelo. I wouldn't have picked her for an angel. But maybe she wasn't the only angel here tonight. Maybe for tonight we were all angels. Why not? Halloween was all about becoming something different.

Justin came over to us and stood waiting to be introduced.

Pestilence looked down at Justin. She was maybe half a head taller.

"Who's this? Nijinsky?" she said.

"Pestilence DiAngelo, my friend Justin Warrener. Justin, Angela," I said.

"Heard some of your poetry," Justin said. "Pretty good."

"Thanks," Pestilence said.

"Heard you once or twice down at the Screaming Bean, too," Justin went on.

"Oh, yeah. That stuff. I'm doing better work now," Pestilence said.

"Think you might have some time to take a look at some things of mine? Tell me what you think?"

Justin was blushing.

"Sure," Pestilence said. "What kind of things do you do?"

"Sort of like yours," Justin said. "Only I usually try to work with forms. Villanelles, pantoums, stuff like that."

"You can write a villanelle?" Pestilence said. "Damn. You'd better take a look at my stuff. I've never been able to finish a villanelle."

"They're tough," Justin allowed.

"Justin Warrener, huh?" Pestilence said.

"Justin Warrener," Justin agreed.

"And you're a friend of Diaghilev here," Pestilence said.

"My best friend," I said.

"And you're jenti," Pestilence said.

"All my life," Justin said.

"Come on," Pestilence said. "I want to see some of the stuff upstairs."

"Sure," Justin said.

They went up the stairs ahead of me.

I had a feeling I'd had my last kiss from Pestilence DiAngelo.

Villanelles? I'd heard of them. But I'd thought they were musical instruments. Or something you could only see under a microscope. And Justin wrote them. He wrote poetry. Justin.

"Boy," I thought. "You think you know a jenti and it turns out there's whole rooms in them that you never had a clue about."

I figured I might as well go up and check out the second floor art. I hadn't really paid attention to it so far.

A lot of it was a series of plywood sheets painted black and gouged with a chisel. They were called scars. *Scar #1, Scar #2, Scar #3,* all around the walls on one side. The tall windows between them were black, too. They looked like they belonged with the paintings.

And then coming up the stairs was the one person I never thought I'd see there, that night or any night.

Ileana. And with her were her father and her mother, the Queen of the Burgundians. And with them was a gray, wispy, elegant little man I didn't know, but he had to be a Mercian. He was wearing the silver eagle on his lapel.

Ileana and her mother came over to me with the little man between them.

"Good evening, Cody," Ileana said. "May I present Captain Ethan Prentiss of the Order of the Mercians? Captain Prentiss, this is Mr. Cody Elliot."

"Good evening, Mr. Elliot," Captain Prentiss said in a sad little voice.

"Are you one of the thugs who beat me and my cousin up?" I said. "'Cause if you are, I've got someone I'd like you to meet. Name's Gregor Dimitru. I think he'll have a lot to say to you. I don't."

I started to go, but Ileana's mom put her hand on my shoulder.

"One minute please, Cody," she said.

"Her Majesty was good enough to give me her protection tonight," the captain said. "Mr. Elliot, I came to tell you that you have won. I have informed the Mercian Order of my decision to surrender to the forces of Burgundy. And I have given the police the names of those whom I believe participated in the crime against you and Miss Stone. Nothing I can say or do will make up for what was done to you. But I want you to know that the honor of the Mercians, to say nothing of my personal honor, has been smirched beyond restoration by what was done to you both. For any of us to attack a marked gadje is beneath contempt. Therefore,

I have informed Her Majesty that we are laying down our arms. I have given the Order my personal opinion that the appropriate course now is for us to disband permanently."

"Gregor is disarming his men," Ileana said at my elbow.

"So that's it?" I said. "War called on account of dishonor?"

"I hope so," Captain Prentiss said. "Frankly, I cannot be sure that everyone will follow my orders. That is why I am here. To be present in the event of an attack."

"So there's still a chance of that," I said.

"Unfortunately, yes," Captain Prentiss said.

"Then I don't think Gregor should disarm anybody," I said. "Not that what I think matters in the wonderful world of the jenti. 'Scuse me." I turned back at the foot of the stairs.

"Oh, Captain? That's my cousin over there. The one your thugs grabbed when they beat me. Just in case you want to tell her what you told me."

When I got to the third floor, I heard steps behind me. I turned.

It was Ileana. She was looking drop-dead gorgeous.

"Cody, please," she said, and held up the key to Gregor's rooms. "Gregor loaned me this. Come in here with me." She unlocked the door.

"What for?" I said.

"I need to ask you some things," she said.

I snapped on the lights.

"Okay. What?" I said.

"Cody, don't you see what is happening? You have won," Ileana said. "This place is open and people are sharing it. My mother is here, and I am here. And Captain Prentiss is here. To join you. After tonight, Crossfield will start to mean something different to New Sodom. We are grateful to you, Cody. All those Burgundians and Mercians who did not want this war. You have saved us from each other. From ourselves. This victory is ragged around the edges, but it is yours. Do you not see this?"

I wasn't quite sure what to say. So for a while, I stood there thinking about it.

"Please, Cody," Ileana said finally. "Say something."

"I don't know," I said. "I don't think I really get you people."

"And yet, if I were ever to do as much for my people as you have, I will be remembered as a great queen," Ileana said.

"I'm sure you will be," I said. "Listen, I should get back."

"Cody, please forgive me," Ileana said.

"Well," I said. "Forgive you for what?"

"For . . . for . . . Damn it, Cody Elliot, you know what for, or you should."

And she started to cry.

I put my arms around her, trying not to notice how wonderful that felt.

After she'd stopped, and blown her nose, I said, "Ileana, I don't need to forgive you. And I don't think you did anything that needs forgiveness. You disagreed with me, but that's just two people disagreeing. Maybe you think you need forgiveness for breaking up with me, but I don't. I mean, it hurt like hell. It still does. But—"

And then she kissed me.

"You were talking too much," she said.

We just held each other for a while.

Under our feet, the music stopped playing. It wasn't the end of a set, either. It was in the middle of a song.

"Uh-oh," I said. "Bet I know who's here. Excuse me."

We went down the stairs and heard voices coming up.

". . . illegal assembly . . . trespassing . . . evidence . . ."

When I got to the main floor, I saw five cops standing by the wigwam. They were surrounded.

"Hey, guys," I said. "'S'up?"

"We don't want to arrest anybody," the first cop said. "We're just here to break this up."

"Break up?" I said. "We just got together."

"Don't get smart," the second cop said. "We know what you're doing here, and we don't want a lot of trouble. We just got orders to shut this thing down like it never happened, okay?"

"But it did happen," I said. "It is happening."

"And it will continue to happen." Mr. Shadwell came over, walking on his hind legs. "Officers, xhere is somexhing unique about xhis night," he said. "A tectonic shift, if you will. Xhe very earxh is moving under our feet as we stand here. Now xhe men who give you your orders recognize xhis, but xhey don't know what to do about it. So xhey sent you to do somexhing about it for xhem. In my opinion, xhey should never have put you in xhis position."

"Look, Rover, nobody asked you," the second cop said. "Back off before you get in trouble."

"Back off from a fight for freedom of speech?" Mr. Shadwell said. "I'd sooner burn my master's degrees."

And he showed his fangs.

He seemed to get taller all of a sudden, or maybe the cop just looked smaller because Ms. Shadwell was standing on the other side of him now and licking her chops.

"Hold on, everybody," I said. "How about if you guys

just arrest me and let the evening go on? I'm the one who cut the yellow tape."

"You lie!" Gregor was beside me all of a sudden. "I cut the tape. Arrest me."

"You damn well did not," I said.

"Actually, it was me," Turk said, coming up on my other side. She put out her hands in front of her. "Cuff me."

"You were not even here," Gregor sneered. "You deserted us. You have no claim to be arrested."

"Arrest me, then," Mrs. Warrener said. "I have an illegal piano over there."

"No, me!" came a voice from the back.

And then everybody started volunteering to be arrested, laughing and clapping.

"Nobody gets arrested," the first cop said. "Those are the damned orders. We just shut this thing down, okay?"

"Not really okay. No," Dad purred, coming forward. "And if you try, I'll sue New Sodom for everything but the sidewalks. And believe me, I can do it."

"Dad, you would? What about Leach, Swindol and Twist?" I said.

"We can't lose this," Dad said. "This has to go on."

Everyone cheered, except Ms. Shadwell, who howled.

"We will not go gentle into that good night," Mom said, laughing and punching Mr. Shadwell on the foreleg.

"Rrrrrrrrr," Mr. Shadwell agreed.

"Don't tread on me," Pestilence shouted.

"Don't tread on us!" Mrs. Warrener cried, and banged on her piano.

"Oh, come on, people," the second cop said. "Give us a break."

Ms. Shadwell howled, and everyone clapped.

"All right, then. We're gonna call for backup," the first cop said.

And he did.

And we all stood around talking about what a great Halloween it was turning out to be, and how there'd never been anything like it, and why hadn't somebody started a center like this fifty years ago, and what would we do next?

And right about then, somebody standing near the entrance to the basement said, "Hey, I smell smoke."

28

I pushed through the crowd over to the basement doorway.

Smoke was pouring out. Fierce, gray smoke, racing up to join us. And behind it I could see the flicker of orange flames.

Fire extinguishers. We didn't have them. Hadn't thought of them. Sprinkler system? That would have been a good idea.

"We've got to get everybody out," I said, to no one and everyone.

I put my arms over my face, went down the stairs, found the door by touch, and slammed it. That might cut off the air supply, I hoped. At least it would buy a little time.

I didn't ask myself why the door was even open.

"My art," Turk said, and ducked back through the crowd. "Okay, everybody, we're getting out," she said. "Everybody grab one piece and take it with you. Save the art. Save the art."

Some people picked things up, or yanked them off the walls. Someone even grabbed *The Scream* from the wigwam. But others just headed for the doors. In a few seconds, everyone was jammed together trying to get out.

"Somebody call the fire department!" I heard a voice say.

"Come on, people, calm down. Line up," the first cop said. "Weren't you ever in second grade? Line up."

But people weren't really listening. The stairs were filling up as people on the upper floors realized there was something wrong. I heard some people scream.

Justin and Gregor thought to open the windows, and people started to jump through them. Ilie and Constantin picked up Mrs. Warrener's piano, twisted the legs off, and rescued it. Blasts of cold air came into the room, and somehow that seemed to increase the panic.

"Cody, come on," Dad called to me. He had his arm around Mom and they were about to go out by one of the front windows.

"Right with you, Dad," I said. Then I pushed my way to the stairs. I was going to make sure that the top two floors were clear.

But how to get up there? People were choking the steps.

"Mosh pit!" I shouted, and jumped for their shoulders.

People yelled, and some of them cursed me, but enough of them got the idea, and I went up on their hands.

I fell onto the floor of the second story, picked myself up, and heard another thump behind me.

"Keep going, Cody," Justin said. "I'm right behind you."

"Check the right," I said, and went left.

It only took a minute. No one was there except for the last people trying to get down the stairs. The dancing had drawn almost everybody down to the first floor before the fire started.

"All clear on this side," Justin called to me.

And we went up to the third floor.

Nobody was there.

"We're done here," I said. "Let's get out."

Then I looked toward the office.

"But first we've got to save Gregor's posters and stuff," I said. "Come on."

"We'd better go," Justin said. "Wouldn't be so good to get trapped up here."

"Oh, we've got time," I said. "The fire's down in the basement, for pete's sake."

"Cody, this is an old building," Justin said. "The wood's dry as straw. Trust me, I live in an old house."

"Five minutes," I said, and tried the door. I guess Ileana had locked it again. "Uh-oh," I said, and leaned on it with all my weight.

"Oh, geez," Justin said. "Let a jenti do it." And broke it down with one kick.

"Thank you," I said.

"Could we hurry, at least?" he said.

"Okay, three minutes," I said.

Down came the posters of Languedoc and the Rheinfells. Justin scooped up an armful of sheet music. I grabbed some notebooks. Everything paper we managed to rescue. But that was all we could do.

Somewhere down below, I heard a dull roaring sound.

The building groaned, and the lights went out. The fire had reached the generators.

"Is it my imagination, or did things just get a lot worse?" I said.

"Unless we have the same imagination, I think we're in trouble," Justin said.

"You know, those windows you and Gregor opened . . . ," I said.

"Feeding the fire now," Justin said.

We ran down the stairs to the second floor.

We were already too late. Justin had been right. I had bought us a few minutes, but the fire was finding its way up the chimneys and along the wooden bones of the old factory. The bottom floor wasn't there anymore. The one we were standing on was starting to go.

We ran back up to the third floor and opened a window. It looked like a long way down.

"We're going to have to dump the stuff, then drop," I said.

I took off my jacket and wrapped it around everything we'd rescued. At least that would probably keep it together. Then I tossed it.

It landed too close to the building.

"Pick that up," I shouted down, and somebody dared to come close enough to get it.

"You first," I said to Justin.

"No, you first," Justin said.

"You're lighter," I said.

"I'm stronger," he said.

By now people were pointing up at us. I saw Mrs. Warrener down there. I heard my mother scream.

And then, hanging on the wall right beside me was a huge pair of wings and a set of sharp fangs.

"Grab on, one of you two idiots," Gregor said.

"Go!" I said, and pushed Justin toward him.

"Get on, Warrener. You can't argue with him. He's more stupid than you are," Gregor rasped.

"Good point," I agreed.

Justin threw his arms around Gregor's neck. They flew into an uprush of smoke and fierce hot air erupting through the windows on the second floor, and they made a crash landing a few yards from the building. Justin picked himself up, but Gregor flopped around like he'd hurt a wing.

Mr. and Ms. Shadwell were under me now, leaping up against the wall, and man, could they leap. But they still only got to five feet below me, and anyway, what could they do?

Behind me, the fire found its way up the stairs. It leapt forward like it was glad to see me.

Then someone very small and dark came arrowing to me out of the night.

"Come, my love," she said.

I could feel her wings working as we dropped toward the ground. I held her tight, and she fought against the hot wind and gravity to set me down gently.

I held on to her until she said, "Cody, let me go. I dropped my shoes."

I released her, and she changed back into her usual self and, shaking like a willow branch, leaned on me while she put her shoes back on.

My jenti princess.

The Daughters were close by, hanging near the Shadwells, who were still wolves. Pestilence saw me with Ileana, raised one eyebrow, and turned away.

Now Mom was hugging me, and so was Dad, and so was Turk, and we were all crying, and Gregor was standing nearby with his arm at a funny angle.

"Is it broken?" I asked when I could.

"No, just sprained my shoulder, I think," Gregor said. "This one"—he jerked his chin at Justin—"threw me off balance."

"Dimitru, you couldn't fly a paper airplane across the backyard," Justin said, and smiled.

"He couldn't fly one across the room," Turk said. Then she wrapped her arms around Gregor's neck and kissed him.

"That doesn't mean I love you," she said.

"I do not love you, either," Gregor said, and kissed her back. When they came up for air, he said, "If you ever go away again without telling anyone—"

"Shut up," Turk said. "I came back. I've never come back before."

And they locked together like a couple of snakes, with Gregor's bad arm hanging off to one side.

Snakes!

"Oh, damn, Mercy's flag," I said.

I pulled away from Mom and Dad and, with them following, I went around to the front of the building.

The flagpole was empty. Maybe somebody had taken the flag down. Maybe the delicate old fabric had caught fire somehow and fallen into the ring of ashes that was growing around the burning arts center.

The fire engines were arriving now. They surrounded the building and started spraying the flames from all sides. The fire acted like it was startled; it seemed to duck its head.

Ms. Vukovitch said, "If this thing was set, I don't care

who did it. I will find them out, hunt them down, and drink them dry. If it was some mistake my boys and I made, I will kill myself."

The south wall let go, burying my sad little corn patch. It was like the flames had been the only thing holding it up.

I felt a hand in mine, small and cold.

"Cody, I am so sorry for you," Ileana said. "It was a beautiful idea."

That was the first time it really hit me that the center was gone. It didn't matter if the fire had been set or not. The effect was the same. New Sodom—old New Sodom—had won.

29

It snowed just before morning. A weak, cold storm that no-body had predicted blew through, leaving behind a thin crust of white. It softened every sound and made things stand out in high relief. It was very pretty. Very sad.

I hadn't slept much. Something about nearly being fried made me feel wide awake. I couldn't stop thinking about the center. I knew it was gone, but I had to know the details. I had to see it. Finally, at about six, I left a note for Mom and drove over to Crossfield.

I know. No license. I'd be in trouble later. I didn't care. I had to see what was left. And after almost getting fried last night, I wasn't too worried about getting grounded. Mom's spiffy Honda was a lot easier to drive than Turk's low-tech antique. And with a scrim of snow on the streets, you can bet I took it slow.

When I reached the bridge, I stopped and got out. From this distance, the mill was a blackened smear against the snow. It looked like it belonged to Crossfield again. Well, it always had, really.

"Well, Mercy," I said to the cold morning air. "We tried."

I got back in the car and drove the rest of the way.

When I pulled up, I saw a tall old man in a black coat staring at the ruin and its necklace of yellow tape. I didn't know who he was, but I had an idea he might be some rich jenti who hadn't wanted the center. Maybe he was the guy who'd set the fire, or paid to have it set. Anyway, he didn't have any business being here.

"Hey," I said when I was close enough. "This is private property."

The figure turned and took off his sunglasses. When I saw those big yellow eyes, I knew who it was, even though I'd only seen them once before, last spring, and that had been in the dark.

"Cody Elliot," Dracula's voice rumbled.

"Rest beneath the shadow of my wings," I said.

Dracula put his glasses back on. I guessed the light was hurting his eyes. But then I realized that he was crying.

"Always you have such silly ideas," he said. "This was a very silly idea. An arts center. To bring gadje and jenti together and do music and painting and words for the pleasure of them. In New Sodom, of all places. Very silly."

Then he hugged me. It was like being hugged by a tree, a very big tree.

"How did you know?" I asked.

"Ileana, of course. We talk, you know. When I spoke to

her and learned that you two were no longer together, I asked her why," Dracula said. "She told me, an arts center. In Crossfield. Where our people were tortured and killed. And she was brokenhearted to lose her boy, but she was very clear. This was not something she could ever accept. But I thought, 'What a mad idea the gadje boy has had. Mad as trying to make his own way in our very hard school. Mad as teaching jenti how to swim. Mad as showing an ancient people something they never knew they could do. Let us see if he has something else to show us that we do not know. So I told her to find out everything as it happened, and to let me know it as soon as she did. I did not tell her why."

"Did you pay for those Dumpsters?" I asked.

"Yes. And I paid Ms. Vukovitch's costs for her part of the work. And for a few other things," he said. "I wanted to help more. But I controlled myself."

"We could have used the help," I said.

"I am not so popular in New Sodom," Dracula said. "In certain quarters, my involvement would not have been welcome."

"You mean with the Mercians," I said.

"Yes. We can see how much difference my reticence made," Dracula said.

"I wish you'd been here last night," I said. "It was great till the place burned down."

"I meant to be. I could not resist. But I booked a commercial flight and we were grounded by bad weather in Brussels. That is the last time I let anyone else fly me anywhere." He threw out his arm toward the mill. "But this," he said. "What will you do now?"

"I don't know," I said. "I don't know what I can do. Look at this place."

The empty windows didn't stare the way books always say they do. They were shut. Shut in pain. Through the gaping doorway, I could see down to the basement and up to the sky.

"Wiped out," I said.

"In any case, you accomplished much, very much. I am proud to know you, Cody Elliot," Dracula said.

"I did find this," he said. "I expect you know the rightful owners."

From under his coat he took out a carefully folded square of cloth.

"It's Justin's," I said. "Where was it?"

"Over there," he said, pointing off toward the river.

I unfolded it.

"It is very old," Dracula said. "See? The grommets wore through in the wind. Probably it tore loose before the fire started."

"Sorry, Mercy," I said to the angel and the twisted snakes. "We did try."

"Mercy?" Dracula said. "Did Mercy Warrener make this flag?"

"Yes," I said.

Dracula held it to his lips and kissed it.

He said two words in high jenti that I knew: "My love."

"She must have been a great woman," I said.

"She was the heart and soul of her people. Their essence," Dracula said. "Their queen."

"She never mentioned anything about that in her journal," I said.

"Journal?" Dracula said. "There is such a thing?"

"Just a lot of scraps of paper she saved over the years for her family," I said.

"I must see this thing," Dracula said.

"It's at Vlad, in the special collections room," I said. "I don't know what it's doing there. It's not even cataloged."

"Is it possible?" Dracula looked up at the gray sky. "Mercy, did you reach out a hand across . . . ?" He shook his head. "I am being foolish," he said.

"Maybe not," I said. "I've kind of had a feeling she's been around, off and on."

"She feels so close," Dracula said, and kissed the flag again. "I asked her to wed me and she said she would do so. It would have healed the wound between her people and mine."

"You must be the Beloved," I said. "In the journal. Every year she remembers the day her Beloved went away."

"Yes," Dracula said.

"So what happened?" I said. "I mean, if you want to talk about it."

"There were no Burgundians in New Sodom then," Dracula said. "I had come on an adventure. To see the New World, and the jenti living in it. And if they had found something worth having, I would lead the Burgundians here and we would seize it. That was my thought. But I met Mercian, and changed my mind."

"Mercy's real name was Mercian?" I said.

"Mercy Ann Warrener," Dracula said. "Mercian. And she was a silver eagle. When she told me she would have me, I felt like I wanted to live ten thousand years, and spend each day of them with her."

"But why'd you break up?" I said.

"The regalia. Her regalia, her crown and scepter, disappeared," Dracula said. "They were most secret and sacred things. They had survived more than a thousand years

241

already. They had survived the loss of Mercia itself. Only two people knew where they were. Mercy and her mother, Queen Susannah. Mercy told one other, myself. When they disappeared, I was naturally blamed. The Mercian militia came. I was lucky and escaped. Most of me escaped."

He held up his right hand, and I saw that the last two fingers were missing. "Captain Danforth was an excellent swordsman."

"And the regalia never turned up, right?" I said.

"No," Dracula said. "Mercy went uncrowned. There were no more Mercian queens."

"I just figured something out," I said. "I think some Mercians believe those regalia are in the mill. Or were."

"Why?" Dracula said.

"The whole thing," I said. "The weird marks Gregor found over one of the storerooms. The fact that nobody seemed to own the mill, but the town wouldn't let us have it. Somebody really, really didn't want us here."

"Come," Dracula said. "Let us see what we can see."

We stepped over the line of yellow tape and went into the ruins.

The fire had destroyed the wooden floors, of course. We could see down into the basement. It was filled with black wood and scorched bricks. The walls that had held the floors up were jagged. They looked ready to topple over.

All but the wall that separated the generator room from the rest of the basement. It still looked pretty strong, because it was twice as thick as the others. Twice as thick except for a slot about three feet wide that was open to the sky.

"Now, that is odd," Dracula said.

We walked out on top of the double-thick wall and looked down into the slot. We couldn't see anything.

"Help me," Dracula said.

Carefully, we pulled the top course of bricks away, then the next, and tossed them down into the debris. Then the next bricks and the next.

And soon we could see it. A blackened wooden box that just fit into the slot.

Dracula gave a cry and forced his huge hands down into the hole. When he had the box, he held it in his arms like it was a baby.

"Come, Cody," he said. "We must open this in front of witnesses. You have your cell phone?"

"Sure," I said.

"Call Justin Warrener. Call Ileana. Call Gregor for good measure. And call your own parents. Gadje should be present."

"Mom doesn't know I took her car," I said.

"Call, friend, and take the consequences," Dracula said. "This is a morning for consequences."

In less than an hour, Ileana was there with her folks, Justin and his mother had come, and Mom, Dad, and Turk were driving up.

"Cody, if you think you are going to get away with what you did—" Dad said.

"Please, Dad," I said. "Kill me later."

"I will," he promised. "In the meantime, you're grounded."

"I need to catch up on my homework anyway," I said.

Gregor came soaring over the river, landed, and bowed to Dracula.

"Thank you all," Dracula said. "I believe this casket contains the lost regalia of the Mercian Realm, things which were lost many years ago, and which I was accused of stealing. It is my wish that all of you should testify later to the contents of this casket."

He laid it on the ground and opened the lid. It snapped off in his hand.

There inside were a silver crown with a double-headed eagle, a scepter with the same emblem, and a heavy chain with another eagle hanging from it. They were almost black with age and tarnish.

"Mrs. Warrener, you will please accept these," Dracula said.

Mrs. Warrener took the box from Dracula. Then he bowed to her.

"Your Majesty," he said.

"Never call me that, sir," Mrs. Warrener said. "These things have caused enough misery."

Everyone was caught in that moment.

"Yes," Ileana said. "It is time for cleansing."

"Indeed it is," her mother said. "Princess, will you not take command here?"

But that wasn't all Ileana did. A few calls, and we started to see Burgundians lifting into the sky over New Sodom and heading our way. Not long after that, Mercians and gadje started to show up in their cars. They came as slowly and carefully as if they were in a funeral procession. But the people who got out were dressed in their grubbies and ready to work.

"You do good work," I said to her as the crowd grew.

She hugged me and kissed my cheek.

"You two are together again?" Dracula asked.

"Yes, Ancestor," Ileana said.

"Good. I am pleased to know that you are not a complete idiot, my descendant," he said.

"Whoa," I said. "You can't call her that."

"Yes, he can," Ileana said. "He is my ancestor. And he is right. I am not a complete idiot."

Then she held a hand out to Turk.

"Ancestor, this is my beloved's cousin, Turquoise Stone," Ileana said. "Turk, this is my most honored ancestor, Vlad Dracula."

Dracula took Turk's hand.

"Ah, the artist," he said.

For once, Turk was too impressed to say anything.

"I asked Cody what his plans were for this ground, and he could not say," Dracula went on. "What would you tell me?"

Turk swallowed and said, "If we could, I'd do it all again. It was the most fun I've ever had in my life."

"Why do you not?" Dracula asked.

"Little things, like it would take a few million dollars we don't have," Turk said. "It'll cost hundreds of thousands just to pull down what's left of this place. Then there's architect's fees, construction materials, workers, legal stuff."

"And there is also the political side," Gregor added.

"I think perhaps that will not be so great a problem now," Dracula said. "I have a feeling something has changed here."

As I looked around at the growing crowd, I had that feeling, too.

"As for the money," he went on, "I will give it, if you will permit me. We might buy the mill next door and get to work quickly. We will see. I am bored with doing the least I can do."

"Wow," I said. It was all I could say.

I went over to Justin.

"Dracula found your flag," I said.

"Pretty good shape for such an old rag," he said, holding it out in front of him. "Maybe we could fly it while we work. Just today."

"We'd need a pole," I said.

"We do poles," Turk said. "Come on, Bat Boy."

"Do not call me that again," Gregor said.

Turk grinned and said, "You prefer Loverbat?"

"I prefer that you spare me your asinine gadje wit," Gregor said.

He took her hand, and Turk shut up.

Quiet and together, they went down to the thicket by the river and came back with a twenty-foot limb.

"Where can we put it up?" I said.

"Permit me," Dracula said, "an old bat's foolishness."

He tied the flag to the pole and lifted himself on his wings to the highest point of the ruin.

The wind caught the flag and it blew straight out.

I looked up at it and gave Mercy Warrener a thumbs-up.

"We did it, Mercy. And I think we're going to do it again."

There was a low roar, and the first Dumpster trucks hauled into view. People cheered.

The cars kept coming all day.

Master Elliot:

This report, while it fulfills the requirements for the course, does not represent a high standard of historical writing. In particular, the excessive personal detail, and I refer here to your frequent references to kissing various persons and how that made you feel, are of no interest to the serious reader.

That said (and it must be said), it is impossible to ignore the facts that, since the events somewhat excessively detailed in this report, the Township of New Sodom has dropped its opposition to your claims of land tenure in Crossfield, a design for the New Mercy Warrener Arts Center has been approved with surprising alacrity, and the financial backing of His Eternal and Royal Highness Prince Vlad Dracula has been secured. As we all know, ground will be broken next week.

Such events can only indicate to the reader who knows of them that you have absorbed the real lessons of this course, indeed of history itself, better than many more fluent writers. I feel no great hesitancy in awarding you a B.

Sewell Gibbon, MA

DOUGLAS REES was born at March Air Force Base, California. He is the author of several books, including *Vampire High, Lightning Time,* and *Grandy Thaxter's Helper.* He has been a college history teacher, a dishwasher, part owner of a ballet school (he can't dance), a storyteller, a hospital orderly, and a number of other things. He now works as a young adult librarian in the San Francisco Bay Area, where he lives with his wife, Jo (the model for the lycanthropic librarian in the Vampire High books), and too many cats.